MW00946135

ISBN: 9781678583262 (Paperback)

Resiliency

The Spirit Within

By

Clayton Malachi Lynch

Special Thanks

First and foremost, I give thanks to you Father God for extending your grip of grace to me daily when I am unworthy of it every day. All that I am is because of what your son Jesus did for me on that cross. -Amen

A special thank you to Grace from EPlus Copy Center in Emmitsburg MD for creating a striking book cover that illuminates the adventures inside the pages ahead.

Thank you Nicole Kramer for helping with photo editing.

I would also like to thank my dear friend Breanne for doing a read through of this manuscript and Denise Henn for editing the final draft.

Finally, thank you, Mom and Dad, for believing in me even when there have been times I could not believe in myself.

This Book is Dedicated to My Wife and Children

Lisa, Isaiah, Joshua, Kaeleb and Lucas

In this life you will stand before many Giants. You might even fall at their feet as I have so often. Yet; through the Spirit of Resiliency, you can look those Giants boldly in the eye and say, "Carpi Diem" which is Latin for Seize the Day! My sons you can become a better person and wiser men than you were yesterday today, because like a river you kept moving forward even when the rain fell. That is my deepest prayer for all of you because I know there will be storms, but I also know there is always light shining through the cracks of the darkness. I have been blessed to be your father. While I am not a perfect father or husband I pray no matter what each sunrise brings you all know I love you very much!

Table of Contents

Part III
Keeper of The Flames

Part IV
Confessions of a Keeper

Part V
Selected Writings and Prayers

"*Clayton Lynch is one of those rare individuals who will not let the obstacles of life stop him from being a success in life. His experiences, throughout his life, have led him to this moment where his message is a powerful one that will inspire you to achieve your goals in life. His story is one that highlights the power of positive thinking, determination, drive, inner strength, and a desire to reach others with a positive message. Clayton's story is a human story and one that will inspire you to break through your own personal challenges to achieve success*"

-Shannon Harvey Gettysburg Campus Vice President, HACC

This Narrative Is Inspired by True Events and therefore, the author has changed the names of characters illustrated within this yarn. Locations and circumstances have been disguised to protect the privacy of all people involved both living and deceased.

Foreword

Life is an ever-changing journey we are all navigating. It is filled with mountains and valleys and for some of us; it seems more valleys than mountains. Clayton does an excellent job using his own life experiences and God-given talents to help us travel through this life. Not only to just "make it through" but to be more than conquerors even during the darkest times that seems to offer no hope. Unshakable joy and peace even amid the deepest pain, hurts and regrets are available to all who will embrace the power and apply the principles that result from acquiring the "Spirit of Resiliency."

It is only through supernatural power we can break free from these burdens and experience true joy and peace. I believe this book can guide you into the place where you can find fulfillment in life despite your past or present situation. Clayton is gifted with the ability to intertwine linguistic melodies with thought provoking wisdom to engage both your heart and mind. Many stories in this book, though heartbreaking also helps us to realize that we are not alone in our struggles. We were not designed to go through this life free of pain and hardship. Rather, we are daily being molded into the individuals we were intended to be as the rough edges are chiseled away. You can become the unique and special person you were created to be and learn to walk a life of hope and victory. My prayer for the reader of this book is that it inspires and encourages you that hope can be found and is available to all who will embrace the changes and commitment needed to be as Clayton describes in this book "Keepers of The Flame.:

Dr. Carter J. Stephan
Chiropractic Physician
Instructor of Anatomy and Physiology
Harrisburg Area Community College

" It's like in the great stories, Mr. Frodo. The ones that really mattered. Full of darkness and danger they were. And sometimes you didn't want to know the end. Because how could the end be happy? How could the world go back to the way it was when so much bad had happened? But in the end, it's only a passing thing, this shadow. Even darkness must pass. A new day will come."

— J.R.R. Tolkien

Introduction

There are invisible dungeons that many people find themselves imprisoned in. Guarded by the Dragons of Fear and Discouragement they are the prisoners of yesteryear and day's long past. This prison is near and far and found in many provinces which map out the vast Landscape of Human Existence. It is a dark abode not shaped by human hands but instead cultivated by humanistic thoughts and feelings of inadequacy and worthlessness. The sturdy walls erected from the Black Diamond Pillars of one's past, pain, sorrows, burdens, mistakes and fear of change gives the impression such walls are unmovable. Those Diamond Pillars sole purpose is to keep the prisoner in that abyss like broken timepieces unable to move forward unless delicately oiled with hope and love itself. Time becomes the very snare of deception they are caught in. So often human nature centers their ambitions on what was lost that they do not realize in their present moment just being there is like a fragile flower opening to the warmth of spring. Take heart and think of such warmth regardless of the current weather.

The deep chasm found inside lucid dreams that become existent when the denser lights of the outside world fade into shadow; separates them from living a life filled with anticipation and joy. Even in their dreams both nighttime and waking, they find no optimism. However, it is in that inner realm where dreams appear that one can discover that hope is a natural, physical and yes spiritual force that moves the dreamer forward.

Self-fulfilling prophecies whispered into the mind's eye of the hostage bound to yesterday by the world and themselves; reveals through the splintered telescope of Fruitlessness a path that can only lead to a life of brokenness and unyielding disappointments. There they are shackled to that belief as their world unravels and drives them into bitterness and malice as they Guard the ashes of ages past. The very reason they stand frozen unable to shake their chains is the only thing certain to them. Again, take heart! For even when it feels like you are sinking in the quick sand of hopelessness, hope is just on the horizon of an individual's Will and determination. The compass is inside of you! It is The Spirit of
• Resiliency and it is in all of us!

This author knows this too well as he discovered throughout the many moments in his life which have sense defined him; that he was serving time in this mind made prison he had shaped with his own memories and wounds. Little did he know that one day those scars would become the very stories he would tell others so they might see that just beyond the horizon of their brokenness there was hope.

It is an inevitable fact that Time while many things is also the very landscape we move through as we journey through life. This very truth is indisputable and beyond contestation. Life is comprised and defined by the moments that shaped or broke us. Yesterday's reminiscences as this narrative will touch upon often; can be dark, cold and when left unresolved a lonely existence. There are often throughout the traveling of that landscape times it feels like it takes every ounce of human strength we have just to tread water long enough to keep from drowning beneath the waves. Yet, again take heart amidst the storm because beyond that dark horizon a brand-new day is waiting but one must believe it to be so.

In a defining moment when this Writer decided that it was time to step out of the ashes, for the first time in my life I could see the infinite spectrum of possibilities that each new sunrise could bring. There comes a point where you find that If you spend long enough in the darkness, you forget what the light even looks like. For those who might have never seen it they continue to fade away like an old photograph buried in a stack of picture albums. Dwindling into the shadows as their light disappears because their past is now like an endless night which shows every sign that there is no escape. It's a lie! The Spirit of Resiliency cleanses the human soul and removes the shadows of everyday life allowing light to seep through the cracks of such darkness.

There is another universal truth that cannot be ignored or evaded regardless of how strong one thinks they may be or even are. No individual can hide from its sharp gaze nor elude its icy fingertips. Everyone suffers or faces adversity in their life. For many people they dance with adversity multiple times and most often they are not the ones leading. Perhaps that adversity comes in the shape of an abusive situation or relationship. Maybe it is learning that a close family member or friend has been diagnosed with an illness or cancer which is irreversible. Sometimes, it is the sharp knife of a loved one who has died before what we might all say, *"was their time."*

Then there are always the sharp words of a loved one that says one day after years of being married *"I am sorry I just do not love you anymore."*

What about the unpredictable hurricane of life that brings the loss of a child or a job. Within the infinite canyons of an addiction the addict finds themselves confined to a "reality of confusion" and it seems unimaginable to escape. They feel as though they bare the weight of the world upon their already crumbling shoulders and there seems to be no hope on the shores of a tomorrow that will never come. Perhaps, a life altering event of an earth-shattering magnitude thrusts upon the soul change that one fears to embrace though in the end they know they have no choice. Again, take heart! For beyond those waves of adversity there is a stunning blue, white, and an extraordinary story of resiliency that illustrates the miracles and treasures found on the oceanfront of a soul renewed.

No one can avoid the obstacles, upsets or curve balls that life is known to and will deliver at varying speeds and undetermined moments in our lives. Those struggles seem to become the reef upon which the ships carrying our hopes and dreams are wrecked and abandon. It is so hard to find the good when you feel like you keep getting tossed against the rocks as you try to keep from drowning in that ocean.

"Where is the light house to guide me to safety?"

we cry out into the howling wind as yesterday becomes the storm in which we are lost. This Author has learned that it is inside those difficulties and unresolved memories of the storm itself that we can find directions. When hope is swallowed by the circumstance, take heart because as evening falls so shall the sun rise.

How does one fight back against the pessimism when it feels as though the wind is blowing so fierce that each step forward is a step and a half back as you are knocked to the ground? This literary venture or better said; ventures which can be found through the pages ahead, proves that if one thing unites us all; it is the threads of hardship and adversity tethered together by both intentional and unintentional strings of circumstance. It is the one thing we all have in common though our outcomes differ as to how we face them. In those moments of circumstance, we can fight back by shaking the dust from the blistered feet of our pasts and live our lives decisively when faced with forks in the road of life.

Every one of us will stand at the foot of many mountains in our lives and come upon moments that throw us off our course challenging our inner strength. Every so often it forces us right to the brink of mental and physical annihilation. Woven with in the fabric of my own life and those mine has crossed paths with; it is without those problematic or even ordinary times there would be no great or extraordinary moments that shape an individual of steadfast character. My mother used to tell me those tests we passed or failed yesterday and today are the testimonies we share with others tomorrow.

As we come to the age of understanding the way the world is; that wisdom illustrates clearly that the scales are always uneven and always will be. Our lives, our individual histories do not differ from the same courtrooms my counselor days took me to when I worked with inner city youth. In America we learned as youths in school that a courtroom was a place where everything should be fair and just. As this manuscript unfolds the stories of those in it validates that real life is not always fair. Good people like Laura, Michael and Layla who lie in the pages ahead die young and criminals sometimes go free. Yet, what is done in darkness will one day come to light. So again, I implore you to take heart because I have been on similar battlefields and stood before such Giants.

From the role of an author I have written about the past before but not in this way. The difference perhaps is that I never looked at what The Spirit of Resiliency was. Through the cosmic landscape of life, we come to find that our scars do not differ from that of old time photography which once required actual film. The central theme found in these pages discovers that it is in the dark rooms of our lives we develop from negatives.

The decades now passed has cultivated the understanding there would be no impactful change without such struggle. The truth revealed later in my life, was that to "break every chain" from an abusive early child-hood to the haunted memories of yesterday and the interactions of those placed in my own life both good and bad; without Christ in me this would be impossible. I discovered almost too late; that the beauty of life is overcoming and conquering what we thought we could not. True joy I found came from knowing there is a God in Heaven whose "Grace Like Rain" gives us strength in the days we are living in. It is through The Spirit of Resiliency I found an inner strength I never knew existed. As Albert Camus once wrote, *"In the depths of winter, I found there lay with in me an invincible summer."*

This concept led me to chronicle the challenges and tests that I've faced in my life and those of the many people I have met. This story differs from any I have written or told because the years have taught me that "it is not all about me." There are those even as I am placing my thoughts onto my computer who have seen worse days than me. I write of such times good and bad not as a boasting tool or to place myself above others but to illustrate the power of Choice, Change and Resiliency. All these years later I still remember like many, maybe even some reading this, focusing mostly on the negative aspects of the situations I was in. It was in those desserts this author was lost and dehydrated in his ability to see beyond yesterday.

For many our pasts, and aspects of it, weigh heavily on our shoulders, barricading us from living a life filled with the possibility of the impossible. I hope this narrative will engage the reader regardless of their spiritual or social beliefs to focus on how our struggles change us and our lives for the better even when it does not seem imaginable. Over two and half decades have passed when this Author finally moved past yesterday and what could not be changed. Once a "Guardian of the Ashes" a Sentry of the past held by the Hands of Time unable to see the potentials of Today, it was through God's Grip of Grace I could find myself "Stepping out of the Ashes" to become a "Keeper of the Flame."

Just as military strategists study the enemy, this Author finds that the lessons found in the arena of life amount not only to pearls of wisdom but also to the benign scar tissue of a mended soul. This is only possible for those willing to embrace the truth that scars are not injuries. Pain caused them yet; they were what were left in the aftermath of those wounds, physical or emotional. They are but reminders of the healing that took place after the injury. I took a long time to realize this myself. I found that wounds alone without healing were the product of not moving forward because lingering in the past kept them infected.

This literary journey on which you are about to embark is unique. One day you might look back and say, "we stood before our Giant's and fell at their feet and while many of us fell at their feet we yelled out to them through the falling rain "Carpi Diem," which is Latin for "Seize the day." Though to the reader only words, it will take courage to complete the journey ahead. Hopefully at the end of that long walk through the jungles of the author's life and the many colorful landscapes of those he has met, you might sit on a beach more beautiful than you have ever known. This author though baring many scars on the battlefield of his soul, found himself through the Spirit of Resiliency millions of miles from the past that once held him captive. He had come to a place that many long for. It is that place when one say's,

"I could stay on this beach forever and be filled with joy I had never known was possible."

Part I

Guardian Of The Ashes

"Life can only be understood backwards; but it must be lived forwards."

— Søren Kierkegaard

Echoes of the Past

This Author has been many things: a pawn, a dreamer, a great architect of the written word, a master of the blade, a hero in some distant and yet enchanted land, but none of these in the way one might think and none of them for more than an instant. Each person's existence is seemingly built around discovering who they are and who they long to become. Sometimes it is when we least expect it that such self-discovery is brought to fruition and made a reality. Occasionally that self-discovery and inner strength can be heard in the distant soundscapes of the past.

Long ago I was once a young child who dreamed of being a well-known poet or story teller that could redefine and cultivate moments in time to illustrate real life. There was and is still something mentally breathtaking about rhyming and uniquely crafted stanzas that seemed to arouse me to pick up my number 2 pencil and jot my thoughts onto my notebook. This was in a time before word processor and computers were the wave of the innovative creativity. Within the pages of a genuine story there comes to life in the mind's eye possibilities one only ever dreamed of. Metaphorical images appearing in color and coming to life on the canvas of the imagination intrigued me and still does. To know those metaphors origins were memories placed in black and white moves creativity in a new and inspiring way; especially when the story is true even if certain aspects must be altered to engage a reader and meet them where they are. How such thoughts, formed out of order inside the writer's mind and comes together in an innovative way while remaining true to the narrative moved me to place into motion those moments that fashioned them.

Writing is an author's thoughts, hopes, and life experiences in an animated motion. The same can be said about the hopes and dreams of tomorrow even if the outcome is uncertain and not yet written because it has not yet been lived by the writer. When I tell an inspiring story or when writing a verse, some days my thoughts are just like cocoons hanging from the saturated branches of creativity in the grey woods of my mind's eye. In time, through the spectacular metamorphous of imagery and innovation those thoughts become butterflies which enter the world in different colors and sizes out of the meadows of printed pages.

This author's earliest discovery about "real life" was when the understanding that the concept of living is filled with many challenges and each person faces them in their own way. What matters is not always the way we faced them but rather the outcome of our choices that makes all the difference. Did we learn anything from those choices? What lessons were whispered into the soundscapes of the mind's eye?

This narrative, while based on actual events has been penned by the willingness though hard at times; to sit quietly listening to the Echoes of the Past murmur softly into the memory sensors of this Wordsmith's brain. Those echoes then move past whispers to become like a Lion on the battlefield of my soul which allow these fingers to type and smith such thoughts into the forge of this tome. While the idea behind the writing in these pages is not to let go of the past but move forward; it differs from listening to the past as a reminder only.

A friend was reading an essay I had written some time ago which was published in a local but well know Community College regarding overcoming adversity. He asked me how it could be written in such a way that when he read it, it was as though he were living the life chronicled in the article. The answer is simple really but does not make telling a story worth sharing any easier because of that simplicity. Whether speaking in front of a large crowd, or writing something inspiring that the author hopes will influence the reader just as the speaker does with their words has a universal theme. I told my friend at the time an Atheist, that the best place to begin is at the beginning. He looked at me as though I just gave him an answer he could have easily googled.

"Really?" He said with a look of utter confusion on his face. *"I want to be able to put my thoughts into fluent words and tell my story. How do I do it like you do?"*

The funny thing is he answered his own question.

"You cannot do it like me and I cannot do it like Maya Angelou, Whitman or even Tupac" I said; though the reference to the rapper might not have been the best choice. I said,

"Everyone has a story to tell and each is different. None are the same even if they face some of the same trials. Beginning at the beginning is writing or speaking about that which you know and have experienced regardless of if it was good or bad."

That unique melody, which can be heard beneath the Emerald Ceilings of Human Autonomy and erected on the Diamond Carved Foundation of the Human Condition, reveals that every story is different and exceptional because no story teller experiences the same exact moments in the same way. This is the very reason I will never say to another person,

"I understand."

While two or more individuals may have endured the same loss or tragedy, or succeed in the same event, how they "Seize that Day" differs based on their emotion's, temperature of the heart, strength of will and even the condition of their immortal soul.

My friend later discovered as I did; that to dim the Echoes of the Past to a point where only whispers of a time now irrelevant to the choices of today, he had to change the way he thought to change the way he lived. To do this he would go through a mental and yes, spiritual transformation which redefined the way he viewed his place in the world, his purpose, and the Truth about where the Spirit of Resiliency comes from. "It is found in Christ Alone."

I share this because many people have asked me how to tell a story that is true and yet inspires and influences without placing too much on the reader at once. Emerson said it best really when he wrote *"What lies behind us and what lies before us are small matters compared to what lies within us. And when we bring what is within us out into the world, miracles happen."*

To understand Emerson's words and what "lies further ahead in these pages" one must listen as the Echoes of the Past serve only as a reminder of the author's world created by memories that have shaped and molded him. The danger as you will discover is lingering in the sinking sands of regret, pain, and sorrow when there is a branch of hope and possibility that comes with change close enough to grab; preventing one from suffocating beneath that sand pit. That hope keeps from fashioning them into an Eternal Guardian of the Ashes.

This Author has found he is nothing extraordinary but rather merely plain and ordinary. The light this Writer now carries inside of him all these years later he tries to bring out when living his life, working, being a husband to his wife, father to his son's, writing, and speaking while believing that miracles happen every single day even if he does not see them. Even when the light inside fades; this Writer must force himself to remember the very moments when The Grip of Grace saved him. Through those Echoes of the Past we discover, may remind us of another time but need not define us. Since yesterday cannot be altered and tomorrow never comes anyway as it is always in front of us, this present moment and the lessons we have learned or are learning, fashion inner strength and resiliency to overcome those once momentous life changing events. Whether we decide to "*bring out what lies within us*" will determine if our story inspires or hinders another.

A writer or storyteller that begins at the beginning and draws upon their experiences will find common ground with their reader as I hope to do with in the many hallways and hidden rooms of this tome. At the end of this narrative's journey I hope those who moved through these pages found the stories with in to become an addiction they couldn't put down. Every person's life in these pages are real and though many names have been altered it has been at intersecting points where our lives collided which have altered mine. A very important question my mother recently asked me I feel led to answer here is this. She said,

"What is your book about, what do want readers to leave with when they ask about how one moves forward and let's go of the past."

While I am now a soldier for Christ I will never become a "Bible Beater for Jesus," I will always when others ask how I broke those chains simply say,

"I can do all things through Christ who gives me strength."

My life will be my declaration of faith. On that same note; one never really let's go, they merely move forward as this narrative will highlight often. Therefore; it will be through the way I live my life as that "Soldier for Jesus" and love for the sinner because I am one too. One other thing I feel led to point out even if others disagree is this. Each man, woman and child essentially brings their past into their present regardless of if they even know it is a choice. The person they lost, the addiction they faced or may be facing, the individual they were, the shame they feel or felt those are all things that will still be a part of them as they move forward. While I talk about letting go of yesterday often I sometimes wonder if "letting go" is a tall tale. I do know that moving forward from the past is not. I along with others in this narrative am living proof of this truth.

Still; I often challenge my own thoughts about that because the myth of "letting go" has left myself and others I know feeling like the healthy way to heal is to shut the door to the past. This Author no longer believes that is one-hundred percent possible because what if and this is a big what if, our journey towards discovering our individual autonomy lies beneath the shadow of yesterday's memories? I do not mean it becomes a crutch but a mere reminder of the very moments that shaped us. It is there on the very edge of Yesterday's Mountainsides that I believe we can find that even in the Chaos and Confusion of our lives, it is those very moments needed for spiritual and human growth.

A troubled youth I once worked with who was from the "The City of Brotherly Love" asked me what inner strength was. It was in the reflections of my own memories I found the only answer I could to his question. It is the very metamorphosis which occurs when someone who was once a Guardian of the Ashes realizes that they can and were, always meant to be Keepers of the Flame. Those who Step out of the Ashes as I eventually did believe that the Echoes of the Past are the voices of Inner Strength and the Spirit of Resiliency whispering into the souls of each man, woman and child, saying,

"Anything is possible,"

While the World in a loud voice is screaming,

"That is impossible there is no changing you!"

Often the reason people drown and are swept in to the undertows of the past is because they did not listen to the quiet voice. Instead they allowed it to be drowned out by the screaming one.

Reflections through the Telescope of Time

I have cultured through becoming a father and a husband that while life is one of mankind's greatest gifts, so is the power that comes with a steadfast faith and obedience to a force not of this world. It is not the human authority that dominate nations or conquers one's enemies in fierce combat. It is not the power of Mother nature that causes mountains to crumble beneath her feet and into the sea. Rather; it is the authority of a loving God whom uses an individual's hardships and trials to make a difference in the world around them and allows them to succeed in the areas of life God has called them to serve in.
Winston Churchill once said,

"To each there comes in their lifetime a special moment when they are figuratively tapped on the shoulder and offered the chance to do a very special thing, unique to them and fitted to their talents. What a tragedy if that moment finds them unprepared or unqualified for that which; could have been their finest hour."

I think often about those words as I realize that my life has presented me with more than one special moment.

Peering in to that deep void of yesteryear through the Fractured Telescope of Time, I can see in the far-off distance floating in the Oceans of Memory, a life once mine. I can visualize so distinctly those very moments I suspect Churchill was referring to all those years ago. Through deep introspection the understanding that each instance, the good, the bad, the somewhere in-between, Life itself "figuratively taped me on the shoulder." When I was a child those showers made of fire rained down upon me penetrating my soul, piercing my mind and placing its hand prints upon my very life. Those "figurative moments" did not seem like opportunity or a chance for anything beyond the understanding of pain, sorrow and feelings of worthlessness.

This Author is reminded everyday through this concept called living and those he has met, that everyone no matter whom they are face many crucibles in their lifetimes. In those ordeals shaped, fashioned and molded from fire and rain they will either destroy us or refine us! Through that metamorphous which was catalyzed by those firestorms, the individual personage that has manifested itself with in the person cannot be denied. It is through that evolution one discovers within them the Spirit of Resiliency.

Honestly it is hard to say what fashions resiliency. Never during this narrative will I claim to be an expert because in all actuality this Author is not. Even now I struggle with such things. It is through the world around me and my small place in it I pen my thoughts on the matter which come from the life I have lived.

Perhaps resiliency is an internal thing that like human emotions comes in many forms and is often obscured from the person built so it makes him or her emotionally strong. Possibly; as this Author will later outline it is more than just the internal storms that all people face which decide if they are built to endure or if that endurance is simply learned.

Regardless, it is the past; the tempests, unbearable squalls, and life altering wakes that help define the future and a person's ability to dictate the outcome of their lives by the choices they make. Even in those darkest of places light can find its way through the concreate cracks of any situation. Still, it is a choice that God himself has granted mankind with that shapes and provides an understanding of the human landscape, the human condition and the fortitude to find one's way through the long cold night of hardship. That wisdom that comes with realizing that the power to choose is influential and essential to the very development of the eternal soul and I now believe is the key to Resiliency. Free will to decide which road one will travel regardless of where they began, I dare to imagine *"makes all the difference"* in determining where one will end up.

Canvases of Grace and Mercy

By chance if you are reading this and are not a believer in Jesus Christ or as some might say "religious" this is not that kind of yarn. Please do not leave just yet. These ideas of resiliency, these experiences uttered through the corridors of the past serve as common ground for many, as I hope my readers will soon notice. This Wordsmith's own life and those in which it has transected with is not fashioned to convert anyone or push unwanted beliefs upon. This Soldier of literary imagery and linguistic melodies believes that through his faith despite where this Author's reader is in their life; they will be inspired by the stories that unfold even when it will be hard to read. That's what true stories and real life are about! The battles we fight every day! It is about the ones we win and lose. To get it right one must recall it all not just what makes them feel good.

As a Christian Soldier later in my life I found that a "religious person" praises God when the sun shines bright and warm. However, a "righteous person" praises God rain or shine. While I am not what I would call righteous when I speak of God; yes, I now believe with all my heart and soul He exists. Therefore; for those who find themselves in oceans of doubt, uncertainty or trapped, perhaps this story will inspire you in your own way and reveal to you how to break those chains which may bind you. In another time this Writer once believed that the only certainties in life were death and taxes. It was not until God revealed that there is hope be on the horizon of this present moment.

Now that I am older and perhaps a tad bit wiser; resiliency is while many things Grace and Mercy etched on the canvas of humanity's souls by God's very fingers. It is His hand imprinted within them forever because of what Christ did on the cross when He gave His own life up for all mankind. There came a time in my "*hot mess*" of a life as a coworker of mine says often, when I found myself wounded and burned to a point of hopelessness. In that dark abyss I *"Cried out to Jesus"* while "*Grace Like Rain*" would one-day shower me with courage and fortitude I never knew I had!

Like an artist who takes colorless images they can only see in the mindscapes of their dreams and brings them to life on their canvas, the resilient individual brings to life the Joy of Living with in their soul. The poet writes of his or her hopes, dreams, perhaps their fears and sorrows. In doing so they take black and white turning their words into people, places and memories the reader can almost feel, hear, touch and smell. It is as if the reader is transported into the very mindscape of the writer no different from virtual reality. I have found that the same can be said of God's creation of each individual whether humanity believes in Him or not. Within each person the Author of the Universe has left his signature and when one can finally read it and understand His love cost nothing they find the Spirit of Resiliency lives in them and they can soldier on through life's harsh landscapes regardless of how coarse the terrain.

The Sword Smith

I am a lover of ancient history and a student of the Martial Arts. Not because it provides me with the tools to cause harm, but the wisdom to prevent it and understand that I am in control of my own choices and my individual destiny. As the great military strategists Sun Tzu, once wrote, *"To win one hundred victories in one hundred battles is not the acme of skill. To subdue the enemy without fighting is the acme of skill."*- Art of War

This Author found through harsh reality that the greatest battles are the ones fought in the mind and soul because it is on those battlefields our fates are truly decided. A man who believes he is going somewhere, will live his life differently than the man who believes he is not. However; the war itself begins on the battlefield of the mind. I am drawn to history and martial arts because the Spirit of Resiliency can be found in the many corners and coves of the subject matter from Sun Tzu himself; to the Last of the Samurai Warriors and even through the life of the legendary Bruce Lee. Yet; it is seen ever so clearly through the Life, Death and Resurrection of Jesus Christ the Son of God in whom I place all my hope.

I often think of how important an ancient Samurai's Sword was to him and how beautifully crafted they were. Have you ever actually seen one? I have not; except in the documentaries I have watched about ancient history. I remember it was one of the few subjects in college I enjoyed and it came effortlessly. Beautiful and uniquely made the swords were. Of all the weapons that man has developed, there are few which lures such fascination as the samurai sword of Japan. To the Samurai of real life, nothing captured and illuminated his warrior's code more than his sword and it was considered inseparable from his soul. Why am I talking about ancient history? What must it do with the Spirit of the Resilient?

When I was in college I did a history report on the origin of the great blades of the Samurai Warrior. The Tales of warriors of old had always resonated with me as I even imaged myself in another time as one of them. The fantasy of such a life would occasionally enter my nighttime and waking dreams which provided an escape from reality. One of my favorite films is still *The Last of The Samurai*. The Samurai's sword was a work of rare beauty and many accounts tell how they were fashioned by the inspired hands of the legendary Musumane who also made daggers.

History found in text books though I dare believe written by those who won their conflicts, seem to still believe that Musumane was the greatest of all Japanese Swordsmiths. When any metal is placed in fire one or two things will occur. Either it will melt and be ruined or if the hands and skill of the swordsmith is true and well trained that simple piece of metal will become uniquely beautiful as it is forged just right with a perfect balance of fire and water as the swordsmith strikes and forms the blade. In doing so placing into that blade a part of his soul alongside his sweat, blood and tears.

I believe that every human is crafted uniquely the same way by the greatest of all Swordsmiths. I speak of the Creator of the universe and the provider of undeserved Grace and Mercy. The one and only God of the cosmos who fashioned the world in place and named every star in the heavens before father Abraham even began to try and count them. The difference between the Samurai Sword and the person is this. The sword feels nothing while the individual feels everything. It is then by choice, he or she can bare the flames of adversity and the hammer of hardship, or melt beneath the pain of individual growth. My mother always said that anything in life worth doing would be hard. This means embracing our scars too!

It is for those who cannot bare it that the Spirt of Resiliency remains hidden away and buried beneath the tainted blanket of humanism and denial for all time. Sure, there are many people in this world who live through horrific things. Millions do not know my Jesus Christ as their personal savior and still appear to survive. In knowing all this; if you are one of those individual's I pray you not let my testimony of what God has done in my life stop you from moving through these pages. Even if you do not see the world as I do, that is ok because I also believe that perhaps after reading my story and so many others you might at least find hope when days seem too dark to weather. You might even whisper to yourself in the mirror, *"what if?"*

I feel it is essential to explain this one important detail that sets those individuals apart from those who place their hope in Christ and those who soldier through life on their own. At the end of the age those who have accepted Him live forever and the joy of the Lord bursts forth from them like a lighthouse in the distance guiding lost ships to safety! That light house's light is seen for miles through the storm and with human existence that light, that joy which "surpasses all understanding" echoes through the years even after the light bearer has faded from this world.

There are many people walking around in the world today alive on the outside but dead on the inside. I used to be one of them. Many of my readers have their own opinions on the matter, their own philosophical ideologies. This narrative was never designed to force change of those philosophies but to inspire readers to open their minds to the possibility of what they once deemed impossible and I am not just referring to Faith, but to the ability to overcome and break free from the chains that bind them.

I am an individual who writes about what God has done in my life. The voices in my head which once told me of my inadequacies and worthlessness because of a past I could not change find themselves with in these pages not to haunt or torcher me, but to recall where I have come from. In my life I found I am merely an illustrator and storyteller of all the lives in which mine has interconnected with and has formed me into the person I am today. This includes the good the bad and the somewhere in between. Those voices of self-doubt have since faded and as I make my way through this narrative I can see ahead the other amazing individuals of steadfast character and those who have seen worse days than me. It is also with a heavy heart I can see and hear the stories of those who remained Guardians of the Ashes. That observation makes it evident this yarn is not just about my life but about what it means to be resilient and swim against the current and riptides of an unpredictable life.

There is yet one more way to illustrate what this narrative is all about before diving deep into that ocean in which I implore of you to follow me even if it means stepping outside your comfort zone. While much of this nonfictional yarn it is based on my own life it is more than that as mentioned moments ago. For I have discovered that I am but a small boat in an immense ocean and like a single grain of sand in a dessert of trillions of other grains purposely placed. You will meet others who have fought and are fighting their own battles. There at the intersection of broken dreams and the threshold where dreams take flight, my path on numerous occasions intertwined and collided with Courageous individuals and the down trodden and broken hearted. On that note; I would like to begin this journey with an antidote I use to tell the troubled youth I once worked with.

The Old Man and His Chisel

In a time long before power tools and machinery, there lived a lonely old man in a distant and forgotten part of the world. Behind his small home a shack really; there sat a massive boulder thirty to thirty-five-foot-tall just off the left side of his land. A thought came to him one hot summer's day; a way to ease his solitude as he had no friends or loved ones to comfort him of an encouraging word.

Grabbing an old chisel which once belonged to his father and his father before him from the old worn table in his small dining room he headed out the front door. As he made his way one hundred and fifty yards to the boulder, he finally stood before that stone and chiseled a way at that massive piece of rock. For thirty years and never missing a day except for the Sabbath one, he worked from the time the sun came up until it retreated beneath the veil of the western skies. An occasional traveler or drifter passing by would laugh and mock him, thinking him insane for allowing his fingers to bleed from the nonstop chiseling of the worthless mountain of a boulder. Still; he did not care and continued to work.

Season after season from dawn to dusk he walked from the house one hundred and fifty yards even though each new year seemed to slow his steps. Then as the sun burned its hottest in mid-summer of the thirtieth year the man suddenly stopped. As he looked up where that boulder once stood, an in adamant object, there now stood a beautiful statue resembling the son he lost thirty-one years before in the wars. It was the first time he had smiled in what seemed an age.

His countrymen and pilgrims passing through came from far away to stand in awe of his marvelous work. Among them were many who had once passed by and mocked him or laughed at him, those who thought him insane for working every day and allowing his health to fade. When they said,

"How did you dream this up old man? How did you make him so beautiful? Look, look he almost looks alive!"

In reply the old man said with tears in his eyes dark blue eyes,

"The statue I did not create for he was always there inside the boulder only hidden away. I just chiseled away at every rough edge until he was finally set free. However, I could not have done it just right unless I was willing to accept that I needed the entire boulder to bring my son back alive."

When we allow God to work on us, to "chisel away at all the rough edges" of our lives through the Spirit of Resiliency beauty from pain, suffering and hardship emerges with such exquisiteness that all the world will look onward in awe even if they do not like what they see. People will laugh and mock that God has such power or patience or that he can take any boulder and make it a beautiful piece of work. Regardless of what humanity and society believes or deems to be truth; that which seemed broken and unrefined becomes an agent of God's power and touches the lives of those who observe His good work and are touched by it. I used to think my life was broken and without purpose. Yet, through every storm and every dark night I now realize that as Albert Camus Once said…. *"In the depth of winter, I finally learned that within me there lay an invincible summer."*

Whispers of Life

The anecdotes we whisper into our own minds are powerful and have influence over our beliefs and sense of value. For me it took a while to realize that I may have involuntarily used my childhood wounds and life experiences to shape and fashion the story I was writing. I allowed the pencil tip of fear to etch many decisions in my life.

Every story worth telling and telling right has an origin but I have found that while one may not decide how a story starts, they have the influence to decide how it will end. More so; not always are those beginnings or ends pleasant. Every yarn of value I trust has purpose and meaning as does every single life despite their past, present or indefinite future. There is that single moment when the very existence of a person's narrative is whispered into the world from the lips of Divine design and intention. It is through that utterance which causes the writing of one's life to appear through the Looking Glass of Time.

Still, what many people do not fathom or perhaps know or believe; is that every life story was being written before Time himself even knew of the adventure. The Great Author of the cosmos himself, God the Father, the Artist and Poet of all our eyes see and ears hear, spoke light into the darkness and the world came alive causing the universe to never be the same. (*Genesis 1:1-3*)

The Wordsmith; who knew each person before they became known to the world had a purpose in mind for the story that would unfold. Like a "choose your own adventure book" from my elementary school days; He allows each character in the story to choose their endings and their own path which if they follow Him or do not will ultimately lead back to Him at closing of the book. What happens after the story ends depends on the chapters written with the ink pen of "Individual Discernment" and is etched intentionally; in the calligraphy of Free Will. I believe that with all my heart and that is why I have chosen and have felt inspired to fashion this narrative. It was somewhere at the crossroads between internally living and dying this truth was revealed.

There is no other way, no other road one can travel, and no earthly trail they can venture beyond that which leads to Jesus Christ can set them free. Unlike the ideologies of society who say all rivers (religions) flow to God, there is only ever going to be one way. Jesus! Jesus said,

"I am the way and the truth and the life. No one comes to the Father except through me." John 14:6.

Many will mock me for what I write right now because to those individuals the Word of God is just another story book. Part of me understands why they might feel that way though. I know a long time ago I did too. However; I have never seen the wind but I have felt its breath upon my back on a hot summer's day as I marched across the hot desserts of Oklahoma and the open country side of Fort Jackson South Carolina after joining the Army.

The breath of the Wind would bring relief for a time revealing its existence. I still remember watching as the Trees seemed to talk to one another on that bus ride home from basic training as we passed through the deepest part of Virginia. While I could not see the wind that made the trees move and sing to one another I could still see the effects of it. I pray those who do not believe as I do still read on because I believe they will still be inspired. Furthermore; I have never seen God as Moses or Elijah did but I have seen Him through the beauty of this earth, the births of my four sons and through the eyes of my beautiful wife. I am getting ahead again so I implore of you to take three steps back with me once more.

Spring 1981

It was April; the spring of 1981 I came into the world and where my story begins. I once heard it said by one of my favorite martial arts actors Jet Li,

"One cannot choose how one's life begins but one can choose to face the end with courage."

I used to believe that my past was my greatest nemesis. He was a shadow cast across my ambiguous future only to taunt and remind me of a broken life destined to defeat me. Shadows are always taller than the person or object projecting them depending on where and when the sun hits them. When our pasts like the sun lingers over us at the slanted angle of futility and time stands still so to speak, that shadow is always at its highest. As the years passed by; I later learned I was wrong. That quick entrance into the world, a moment, a blink really, acquitted me from the reality that was life. In that spring of 1981 I was born with chocolate colored skin, the rich creamy kind some might say. As for my ethnicity it is unknown even to this day. I only mention my skin color because my flesh was often stained with bruises from an abusive mother. "Accidents" happened often just as dry lighting has started forest fires in the mid-west and on the west coast. There was no telling when the lighting would strike.

My hair was once like fine black silk curled and thin, while my glassy eyes were brown and glazed over with a vagueness that could not be named. Age has since removed that curly hair but faith has filled my eyes with a light once not present. Before that light, the unquestionable existence of fear, loneliness, and brokenness peered out into the world through those two tiny gateways to the soul. I never knew I had a soul or there was a God until many years later.

I was the kid from the wrong side of tracks before I even knew I was. It is sometimes hard to remember life back then as only flashes appear here and there. I am certain there is much God has allowed me to forget. At the very tip of memory's oasis where resides unforgotten dreams; I see those early years when I lived in a trailer nestled back away from the main road which was obscured by the trees along the narrow drive way. The hidden trailer also veiled that underneath that rickety old roof lived two brothers. From what I can now vaguely remember from those waking dreams which were once reality was living outside of Historical Gettysburg in that rundown trailer beside the old railroad tracks.

Every night at an unrecallable time the whistle of the old freight train would let me know that the sunrise was near. Sometimes the silhouettes and shaded figures fashioned in my mind's eye haunted me. Hidden beneath a blanked of dreamlike whispers, I could almost hear the darkness laughing at me as the soft voices in my mind called out to me from the hidden crevices of nightfall. Even as an older man I would hear those undertones in the wind occasionally. The same war fought on those bloody battlegrounds only a few miles up the road in July of 1863 would be fought in my own home. Not by cannon fire or piercing bayonets, not with the devastation brought forth in the aftermath of a Union or Confederate Battalion trying to gain some ground; but with an arsenal just as damaging and no General to prepare the troops for war. The cadences of domestic violence and abandonment would be heard through the next few decades as they were played upon the fragile snare drums of my memory.

Those who have Seen War

In the movie "We Were Soldiers" that dialog at the end of the film cuts deep in to a person's soul. Journalist Joseph Galloway says...

"We who have seen war will never stop seeing it, in the silence of the night we will always hear the screams. So, this is our story…."

I imagine this could be worded for those who have been through what I have or have seen worse days than I by simply stating….

"We who have been burned by abuse and neglect will never stop feeling it, in the silence of the night the cries we were too afraid to let out are heard with in the walls of our memories and buried deep within our mind. So, this is our story…"

So, to tell this story right I must be honest, there will be times you will want to look away and not read. Maybe even in these first few pages this has happened. Perhaps you did so not necessarily because you feel bad for me but because you know of someone I speak, maybe it is you. Perchance, through the pages ahead you might see the wax images of yourself from ages past glowering back with that uncanny look of recognition. Please do not cry for me or feel bad because these moments have led me to become the man I am through the discovery of my own autonomy and God's presence in my life.

It is because of each interaction and all the wrong turns where *"two roads diverged in a yellow wood"* as Robert Frost would say, that I can pen these thoughts and share them. I now realize that it is those very moments in time that *"have made all the difference"*. No... do not feel for me feelings of sadness but I pray you develop and atmosphere of empathy for those whose stories are unfolding right now the very same way so that perhaps courage will ignite a flame within you to be a voice in their silence.

This author's true desire is that you my reader can stop what I am about to share from being the story uttered through the existence of others or maybe even your own life. Maybe if you are trapped yourself, in time or you know someone who is, you can become more than just a Guardian of the Ashes if you will.

It might be expressed through the many philosophies and understandings of the wise, that a Guardian stands watch over faded years. They are merely living statues held tightly by the grip of Time himself like toy soldiers in the hands of a child. They are Sentries of the black and white writing on the torn and discolored pages of their lives. The intense wounds of yesterday's pain are all but extinguished and only the ashes of memory linger, reopening them often by mere recollection. Rather than move forward and into the immense possibilities of tomorrow they loiter and hold on to what cannot be changed. Therefore; each day they relive moments that no longer physically have sway over them, but internal wounds that never healed hurt worse than the day they had gotten them and it eats away at their souls. Those ashes, those reminiscences serve as agonizing souvenirs of another time when autonomy and individuality was stripped from the person who has now become a Guardian.

"In the depths of winter" the Guardian beats the drums of Defeat to a cadence slow and somber because they have lost all hope. There that is it! Hopelessness in one simple but powerful word is the very definition that is The Guardian of the Ashes. Around that corner beyond yesterday's dangerous mountain side; it is there at that messy intersection where Hopelessness and Hope converge, this Author finds that Hoping in the Darkness is a complicated and yet delicate thing. Throughout the very fabric of life, wisdom reveals to those willing to listen that we live in dark times but that need not be the story we will tell. The Guardian of the Ashes comes to believe that the darkness they know is the way of the world and is the way things will always be. If only they would believe there is no truth in such a belief unless they will it so.

From the lucid dreams and memories of this ordinary writer born into an uncertain life there is something problematic with living in a world of darkness. The Guardian of the Ashes eventually loses hope there is anything other than the darkness. On the battlefield of the human soul without resiliency hope becomes lost and dead. I have cultured through the years you need not know what is right to be responsible, you need only to do what is right to be responsible. Often that will take courage beyond what many believe they have with in them because of the changing world we live in. I mean after all sometimes what is wrong is right and what is right is wrong. That obligation requires an individual to become a "Keeper of the Flame" so their light will grow and offer hope found in the resilient soul.

Throughout my life I have learned that we all are like the stars of heaven. Each person is individually and uniquely made. They are fashioned by the hands of a jealous but loving God. Identical to the lifespan of each star in the whole of the cosmos we too will one day burn out, but it is that responsibility and courage that helps the Guardians step out of those ashes breaking free from the Hands of Time and move forward. That action of stepping out of the ashes to become Keepers of the Flame is the very definition of the Spirit of Resiliency. In doing so they let that light shine for all to see. Though they may look back occasionally as I have been doing to tell this tale, they no longer linger there or tread in the oceans of the past where most do and drown from defeat.

So, what set me on the path to becoming a Guardian of the Ashes? It was an early age really. Perhaps it was three or four. I too was once a Sentry of the past as I can remember how I had become acclimated to physical abuse to where no tears would flow from my eyes. In my hand I once clenched glass and though the blood flowed from my hands there were no tears to accompany it. Why I even did that I do not know to this day. All I know is that I was once broken but aren't we all somehow? As this narrative will reveal later through the reflections of the many troubled youth I once worked with, they would say,

"I just became numb Mr. Lynch."

I knew that feeling!

Though I forgot it, at one point early in my life I had been dropped on my head rupturing my left eardrum and fracturing my left femur. Maybe that is really where my Guardianship started. It is that which I am sure has contributed to the hearing loss and continued nerve damage in my left ear along with my later years in the Army.

My biological mother was perhaps a "lady of the night," standing at 4ft 11 maybe 5ft and she would be the one my memories recall initially sending me into the first of many crucibles guiding me to the gates where for a long time I would become that Guardian I spoke of earlier. Those flames would rob me of my childhood innocents if there is such a thing. What she looked like I cannot recall. Funny though, one of my favorite poets who endured similar ordeals and the author of _I Know Why the Caged Bird Sings_ said,

"I've learned that people will forget what you said, people will forget what you did, but people will never forget how you made them feel."

I wish I could have met Maya Angelou I think we would have been such good friends. So, while I may not see the appearance of my biological mother anymore because her face is no longer recognizable; I use to feel every day the way she made me feel, broken and without purpose merely an adamant object. I can recall dreams of seeing her in the mall, on the street corner, and sometimes in the darkness of the nighttime staring at me from my bedroom closet and blaming me for the choices she had made. Her glare seemed to say the words,

"Clayton everything you claim are all the fabrications of your own mind."

I know I saw her in my dreams long ago and that is all they were but they were so real it was scary. Then as the years passed; only a silhouette of her remained imprinted in my memory as Time erased her face from my mind. There were nights I often doubted what those dreams revealed. What was real? What was not? It was as though those words from that one dream were being played back like a broken record.

When the men stopped arriving I became an object, not a child, not a son, an object expendable and disposable and subjected to sexual exploitation. There is much more that the years or perhaps God himself has barricaded and hidden from me behind the stone wall of elapsed dreams that once haunted me. For that I imagine I am grateful.

As for my biological father he is a nameless man inside that splintered chasm of yesteryear, a drifter perhaps, a one-night stand, possibly he may be someone I have passed on the streets all these years later. It is even possible he could have been a coworker and I never knew it. He was a name on my birth certificate with no certainty of its validity. Who he was, where he was from will forever remain locked up, obscured like the mysteries of space and time itself in an invisible chest never to be opened by earthly hands. I suppose that is a good thing.

So, what is the best way to define "numbness?" Hmmm... Through the lenses of a now grown adult it is a lot like a solar eclipse. The moon passes between the sun and the earth, blocking the sun's rays for a time, hiding it to be precise but the truth is it is still there. Numbness is the unconsciousness of the emotions (sun) we are supposed to feel. I don't know I guess that is one way of looking at it. What if it is better defined as apathy because to reveal those emotions will not change the past? At some point I knew what was going on whether that was physical, verbal or sexual, you just feel nothing anymore. You become a living shell hollowed out by circumstances not always in your control.

Rolling off the tongue of days gone by the linguistic murmurs sung through the soundscapes of now distant dreams tell stories of a time when my brother and I were left alone in a trailer for five long weeks. How we survived I can only imagine was the hand of God reaching out of the Cosmos and providing direction as we lived on molding bread and water. Though four and half maybe five years old I knew that to live one must eat and I tried to make sure my brother lived not understanding the significance of that knowledge. So, it was that our lives should have probably ended there but it did not.

Much more could be said about those years that no one remembers except for a forgotten few. I found that Time is an evil comedian really and a song writer of lies as he tries to persuade all who dare to listen. Singing upbeat songs that's lyrics articulate to those who will listen through those false verses and stanzas he will always be their friend and that "Time Will Heal All Wounds". If this were true more about that spring and proceeding years could be uttered, but Time would not allow every detail to be shared because he knows he cannot hide the truth. Time is also the dreaded history teacher who gives out his exams before teaching the lesson. The Spirit of Resiliency I would realize years later taught me that memories never seem to slumber if we remain hostage to the past and if we choose to become a Keeper of the flame or not. Instead those memories are the very archetypes that seem to act as dream weavers reminding us of another time when life was good or bad.

Shattered Silence

A short way down the road from our rundown trailer lived a teenager going through some of the same things we were. Looking back though I now imagine his situation was much darker than mine. Only God knows the details of that tragic yarn and it would not be mine to tell. What this Author does know is that he was the son of our landlord, the same man who once entered our trailer one evening intoxicated. On that night, seasons a million miles from my memories rest stop, he pushed me into an old kerosene heater leaving behind a scar I still bare on my left hand. The landlord was a tall man whose skin was dark as shadow with eyes I can still remember even as I type these words. They were tinted with shadowy hues of malice, coldness and glancing back even subtle hints of sadness. He was an older man perhaps in his late fifties but time has this way of distorting and confusing recollections. That night was just over three and half decades ago.

That scar I bare was just another reminder of where I have come from but no longer an indicator of where I am heading. One dark summer night as the old man slept passed out from the alcohol coursing through his blood stream the silence was shattered by the sound of a shotgun penetrating the night and then carried swiftly upon the back of the wind as it echoed through the trees, down the lane and through the trailer park. For a moment, time slowed, and the sound of an approaching storm forged with in the human soul was all that could be heard. I will not say his name for that is not important nor will I mention the old man's.

All I know for sure is that on an evening with no stars or moon illuminating the sky, there were only shadows in the darkness. In an un-remembered month or year, the revengeful thoughts of a beaten fifteen-year old seized that teenagers mind with a grip of fury. Upon pulling the trigger; came the hot breath of death and the serrated knife of revenge. I imagine a new-found fear of the future had also manifested itself in that young man's mind.

The boy was picked up by the police and no one knows for sure if it was him that told of two small children left alone for five weeks in a trailer up the way from where his father now laid dead. What I can say is I remember him, the teenage boy that is, vaguely and always in a decent light, despite his actions. Before this night sometimes he would come and play with my brother and me. You see he was broken like me, and at some point, the wind blew too hard and he just gave in.

It was soon after that children services and youth removed us from the home and the judge eventually declared us Wards of the State. We joined the many of children in American Culture taken from dire situations and when you say,

"*Ward of the State*"

it was like my brother and I almost sounded like someone's property rather than humans. However; that removal/intervention could have been the very intersection with in our past that decided whether we would live or die. Again, over three and half decades have passed like a goodnight's sleep and I have discovered that my becoming a foster child was a gift! You see I was chosen by someone, I was wanted even though back then I did not see that as clearly as I do today.

Flowers and Weeds in Concrete Gardens

A person has the ability for a time to appear on the outside strong and together even unmovable, while on the inside the walls are caving in. For me I felt like one of Peter Pan's Lost Boy's even though back then I had never even seen the Disney movie or even heard the story. Sometimes, we ask,

"Who am I?"

or the famous one I used often without realizing it,

"Why?"

I found later as time marched onward that some people wear masks for many reasons. However; I would wear a mask so others couldn't see the truth that would become for a moment my life or the sorrow in my eyes.

In a small town known for its history and its tourism the brochures left out the broken and forgotten lost boys and girls of Adams County. They were the many children who were flowers and weeds growing in concreate gardens and along gravel walkways. Their life spent struggling to be seen through the cracks of "normal" society. Through the eyes of the Foster Child, the kid in a blended family, or the neglected the future was uncertain as to if they would bring beauty to the world or continue a cycle of brokenness and violence. Just as "Every Rose Has Its Thorn" every individual growing in the gardens of abuse and brokenness was a torn piece of fabric from the quilt of society.

It is from the cracks in that concreate garden of child-hood youth this Author discovered however this is not just the case in that historical town but in every single community across the United States of America and even to the ends of the Earth. I think of that Jason Michael Carroll song "Alyssa Lies" about the little girl who went to school every day with bruises and one day she just was not there anymore. While I am alive and stronger than ever those words,

"Alyssa lies with Jesus because there's nothing anyone would do"

could have said,

"Clayton lies with Jesus because there was nothing *anyone would do."*

In every city and town in the very neighborhood my readers live, there are those unable to bare the flames and not because they do not want to but because they never even had the chance. In those communities whether it is a wealthy neighborhood or a poor one; live lost boys and girls who long to just be wanted and loved.

Then one day you wake up fifteen years later and you realize there is no such place as Neverland. There is no magic pixie dust that will allow you to fly away just by thinking a happy thought. Even if there had been what happy thoughts would there be to ponder? Peter Pan's Neverland cannot be found on any map and it isn't the *"second star to the right and straight on to morning."* The places we take ourselves to escape we find are only momentary voyages from reality. Like all voyages at some point we must dock and set foot on dry land and, that would be the real world where people must decide who they are and who they will become.

Scars of the Guardian

My younger brother would often ask me why I would not let go of the past. I guess he was asking me why I allowed myself to go back into the flames of yesteryear long after the fire had been put out. He was asking perhaps why I remained a "Guardian of the Ashes." Was it really, out? The fires that scarred me on the inside of my soul that is. Who knows, maybe the coals remained illuminated by the heat of finally understanding the reality of what had transpired. The smoldering of suppressed emotions perhaps drove me there. I used to argue with him I had let go, but deep down I knew this was one thing he had been right about and I was in denial.

I now believe it is because while wounds to one's flesh often heal, scars remain inside where no other human can see. The difference for me these days is I now trust that "*my scars tell a story. They are a reminder of times when life tried to break me, but failed. They are markings of where the structure of my character was welded*" as Steve Maraboli and perhaps many others once said.

The scars of the Guardian and the resilient alike are always there on the lightly lit embers of one's past. They are covered in the ash left behind by the fire of life's uncontrollable injustices. Even the controllable challenges and individual decisions wrongly made serve as the tools in which those scars were cultivated. Still; as I have mentioned often those ashes are no more than the vestiges of perhaps failure or on the other side of that coin, what an individual endured and overcame. I suppose that is why I do not linger there but remember it occasionally.

I once told my brother years after he asked me that first question, "*I do not tread in the oceans of yesterday because I know it wears a man down and eventually he will drown.*" I believe that now as sure as the sun rises because I nearly sank below those waves myself. It is now that I consider every fiery forge we are placed in whether of our own doing or that of another is never useless if a lesson is learned. It is that ideal which pushes me to believe one can soldier onward into the storm and weather it with courage.

I do not recall when it was, perhaps; when he turned fourteen my son asked me,

"*Dad what makes a man a man? How old do you have to be?*"

Looking at him while asking God in my heart "*what did I do to deserve such a blessing*" I said,

"*It is any age when you are able to take ownership and responsibility for your actions without blaming others. A man owns his choices and has integrity regardless of the whether he has done something bad or good. I think son that it is understanding in difficult moments and times of our suffering, whether playing sports or in living we learn from them.*"

As we continued our drive that Sunday making our way back from church he said,

"*What did grandma mean when she said you have been through a lot?*"

So many questions and I worried about what he would be asking when he turned eighteen.

"Someday I will tell you but for now be a kid because if you blink you will miss it. Sometimes I feel like I did" said with a smile.

I guess what I was trying to tell him but knowing he would not yet grasp the complexity and yet simplicity of his question was this. We will in our lives stand before Titans! More so; will fall at their feet. However; whether man, woman or child those who will and have emerged the strongest most resilient souls are tattooed with beautiful scars.

"From the Ashes the Phoenix Can Rise"

No man, woman or child can emerge from firestorms fortified if they have been thrown into or entered that cauldron of their own accord without someone to come alongside them. I believe now that God places those individual's in our paths and we might even become the crucible they face. My mother; the one who "chose" me and loved this beaten and weary ship taught me about the Spirit of Resiliency.

Over the years through my journey and longing for self-discovery, I have found this to be an inventible truth. Even though I failed chemistry and got a D- in biology; anyone one by natural laws of human ecology with all working parts can create a child but not all can raise them.

"Children are a gift from the Lord; they are a reward from him" the Psalmist writes in chapter 127:3. However; there are so many people in this shadow torn world whom take those rewards and discard them as though they were not of God but of their own creation.

She, who I now call my Mother, saw me not for what I was, or what I was doing but for who I could become. She walked through "fire and rain" herself and through my observations of how she lived her life and trusted in something she could not see but felt; helped refine me into who I have become and who I hope to one day be. I watched as her first husband treated her like she was nothing more than an object when she had become everything and the only person who seemed to care if my brother and I were together or even if I lived or died both in body and spirit.

There are two very important things I learned early in my life. First from my biological mother, I did not want her legacy to be mine, even though I did not know that word or even what it meant until all these years later.

Second, my new mother's first husband taught me how not to treat women or people. I remember "the way he made me feel too." A man whom though I never heard him say it, did not care for my skin color, the way I looked or the outcome of my tomorrows, continued a cycle I knew too well. A cycle cultivated in violence and anger. Yet; no matter what he did I did not let the tears come, they were not there until one day I saw my mother crying.

"Why is there water coming from your eyes mommy, you are leaking,"

I uttered from my five-year-old vocabulary. I cannot even remember why she was crying only that it was the first time I think I connected tears with emotion. An emotion I did not understand or know how to express.

When I was a child I was fascinated with mythology and other stories of fantasy. In another time when I liked to read I would escape into those tales and become part of the story. When my mother's first husband would punish me for what I cannot remember to this day by making me run in place as he would bring his fist down toward my feet, I retreated to a place where men could fly and run at incredible speeds. Upon the backs of flying creatures and other winged horses they would soar off on adventures that would make them legends among men. Upon their return crowds would cheer. When I did this, I could run as the wind blows for as long as needed.

One of my favorite classes in College beside history was Greek and World Mythology. Every great mythological tale told of demi gods and goddesses' resilient spirit. I did not know it was a real thing. On that same note; I did not know what courage was, nor did I acknowledge fear because for me the outcome of reality was always the same. Therefore; behind that solar eclipse of sentiment and emotion I hid myself. Who would have thought that Aries himself metaphorically speaking would rage inside me as war waged from obscured anger could no longer remain; behind the numbness I once understood.

My favorite story was that of Perseus the mythological Demi God and son of Zeus. Cast off into the sea with his mother who did not survive a coffin; he is rescued by a fisherman who raises him as his own. Perseus and I just seemed to have so much in common, except my coffin were my memories, and my rescuer a music teacher from Western Pennsylvania. The other significant difference I imagine is that his story; was make believe and he became a hero to his people a champion and defender of justice in a war-torn land. Where I am headed on that front I do not know, but I have prayed every day that the real God, not a mythological one, but the Father of my friend Jesus Christ might lead me in my own time and reality to be a champion of the faith and my life a testimony of his Kingdom. I know many days I fail him in that arena.

Time does things to an individual and much like an Alzheimer patient it robs an individual of those things that brought them perhaps the little joy they might have found. For some it takes away the abundance of joy they carried and they become nothing more than a walking shell emptied of life from the inside out. I realized as I struggled with memories I obscured for a time, that in everyone's life; everything buried surfaces. Just like a lie,

"Everything done in darkness always comes to light,"

my mother would tell me. When it does a person either crumbles beneath the marble ceilings of that truth or as Egyptian Mythology would have it "*From the Ashes the Phoenix Rises*" and they find they are that Phoenix reborn with new purpose and meaning!

Why the metaphoric illustrations of a Phoenix rising from the ashes of a broken and shattered life one might ask. As one who found mythology fascinating regardless of what part of the world it bared its origins, the phoenix has been a persistent allegorical symbol throughout the ages and across the wide expanse of different cultures. Its symbolism echoes through the hallways of humankind's imagination and touches the boundaries of reality with its fingertips of realism as it relates to being reborn. Despite such diversities of societies and changing times, the phoenix seems consistently described as a bird with brilliantly stained feathers, which after an extended existence, dies in a fire of its own creation only to rise again from the very ashes of its own demise. Its own making...... being significant to the reality one comes to when they realize all those stories I myself once believed in, were only stories, and that I had to become the author of my own story in which the real world was not one where I could merely escape and survive.

So, if my comparison of personal autonomy in correlation to that Phoenix is merely a literary symbol, it can be agreed this mythical bird's illustration of death and rebirth seems to resonate in the caverns of humanities' aspirations and serves as an outline for the Spirit of Resiliency. It does not differ from when an individual accepts Jesus Christ as their personal Lord and Savior. Jesus himself explained to Nicodemus when he said in John 3:5-8,

"Very truly I tell you, no one can enter the kingdom of God unless they are born of water and the Spirit. Flesh gives birth to flesh, but the Spirit gives birth to spirit. You should not be surprised at my saying, 'You must be born again. The wind blows wherever it pleases. You hear its sound, but you cannot tell where it comes from or where it is going. So, it is with everyone born of the Spirit. (NIV)

Therefore; this author found that through Christ and the Spirit of Resiliency, the realism of facing the flames and the forges that soar upon the wings of yesterday's circumstances becomes more evident as a person understands that they must either endure or allow themselves to turn to ash. It also determines if they will remain "Guardians of the Ashes" whose fear of yesterday will cause them to linger where they are standing guard over a past that cannot be altered, or if they will one day become "Keepers of the Flame" who's light burst forth from the darkness with such intensity that the darkness cannot contain it.

A Safe Harbor in Life's Storms

Many believe that DNA and an individual's origins define them but this is a fabrication. It is a great lie conceived with in the mindset of humanities many quests to know the answers to life including its meaning. This Author has found that Societies definitions and explanations also are not always candid and the era in which we live does not define right and wrong. Moral or immoral right is right, wrong is wrong and moral is moral regardless of the majority vote or consensus.

I spoke of my foster mother but in all reality, was and will always be my mother. She has been now for the past thirty-three years. So, for a moment I will define what a mother is. For one it is not always the person whose womb we spend nearly nine months in before being introduced to the world, sometimes it is one whose skin, genetics and origins differ from our own as became my case So, from this point when I speak of my mother the word Foster will no longer come in front of the Noun Mother, because the woman who raised me, that music teacher from Western Pennsylvania will always carry that title.

As you will discover in pages ahead and may have caught brief glimpses of, a real Mother's Love for her child is like an atoll or island in Life's immense ocean. It is a place I believe regardless of the weather, despite the traveler's (child) choices, relics a peaceful, quiet shelter from the unyielding and ever-expanding drift waters in a violent world. It is a safe harbor absent from the ridicule and abuse I once knew. For the broken heart and down trodden it teaches the sailor that all vessels get thrown around and battered against the boulders and rocks of Life but that love is unconditional because it is a choice. For me though many years of fighting and arguing would transpire because of my own naïve mindset, my mother was like a Citadel on a Mountain made of pure Diamonds as it has been believed to be the hardest and the most incompressible material on earth. It is unyielding and steadfast! In that stronghold I was and have always been able to find protection when the Waves of Yesteryear's memories and the storms of present day seemed to drown me in hopelessness and uncertainty.

These days when I am asked what my mother has taught me I always think of the one who took me in and chose me when DNA and abuse abandoned me and essentially left me to die. I felt this important to share and I am hopeful mom you are reading this because if ever a day comes when you look back on your life wondering what differences you made, I hope you see in that telescope of your own yesterday that your love for me despite the hardships and those you faced that were not caused by me was always like a beacon illuminating bright with Faith and Prayer. It is the same light house if you will that I hope my children and those I love and meet see shining through me when days seem dark.

My mother taught me that through the shifting tides of an unpredictable life a mother's love, discipline and above all encouragement ensures their children that no matter what life deals out we can find a safe harbor regardless of tainted roots or biology. I am sure my mother will come up again as much of who I have become and my ability to Step out of the Ashes of the past would not be possible without her in my life.

"Music Makers and Dreamers of Dreams"

In my youth I was not good with sharing how I felt because I did not know what I was feeling. Trusting another eluded me as well because the reminders of the past would eat at my soul. Even now at thirty-eight years of age "the struggle is still real." The difference between then and now is long ago I was emotionally not very intellectual. This is not me calling myself "stupid," it is merely observing that I could not identify what I felt. At my current age this is still a chore.

It seems like only yesterday my mother gave me an old Bundy cornet, the little brother to the trumpet. It was an old thing not very shiny and scarred with dents from faded years but it still had a beautiful sound. It was perfect really because those scars and dents meant we had something in common. I later learned that the horn did not make beautiful music but the musician holding the horn did. I would find myself taken in by the classical jazz and big band sounds of another era in time. Just like the old musicals I love like *Singing in the Rain, The Sound of Music*, or even *Grease,* I could imagine myself as one of the characters. For some unexplainable reason I could just hear it, the "Sound of Music" that is and then I could play it. Sometimes I saw myself on Bourbon Street or a small stage in Olé New York City just like in the old movies.

The ironic thing is the first song I can remember playing was "*It's a wonderful World*." Perhaps, it was because I dreamed of such a world where yesterday had never happened or the day before. When I took lessons, I found counting the measures and notes challenging, but man could I play that horn and I loved it! It was a new place to go and unlike those Demi God's and Goddesses or flying horses the music still lives on inside me today more refined and fluent. Another inner innovation concealed beneath the reflecting lake of my feelings was an emotional connection with Ray Charles and Louis Armstrong both talented men who endured many trials and hardships in their lives but overcame their struggles through music. With each day that cornet became an amplifier of the emotions I could not name. The notes clearer with each passing season until many years later I would one day play for falling soldiers, police officers and even stand on home-plate at Camden Yards Stadium which I will visit later in the final section of this narrative.

The first time I watched Willy Wonka and the Chocolate Factory, I still hear the echo of Gene Wilder uttering the words;

"we are the music makers and the dreamers of dreams."

Now that I am older it makes sense and it is more than just a great movie line. It isn't even just about music. The underlining meaning seems to say that action makes the realities we dare hope for and that dreams are carried out by those who will endure because any musician knows that practice is not without its challenges but hones the artist's craft. This truth applies to any artist. Therefore; perhaps any expedition worth taking in this life will be demanding and not without its encounters. A life deprived of the Dreamer's experiences whether good or bad can produce no music worth playing or hearing regardless of what disguise or talent it comes in.

Music I have learned is one of God's greatest gifts next to his Son Jesus, that mankind has been given. Even today over thirty-five years later I pick up my horn, close my eyes, oh...my weary eyes and allow my fingers to move, my mind to let go, so the music will speak of what is inside and it does my heart good. It is like speaking another language and it is liberating.

This Musician has come to a steadfast understanding that resiliency is not something someone can learn in a text-book; it is not easily taught because it is internal and often revealed only through circumstances and the touch of Adversity's hands. Few people grasp the reality it is there. Yet, I still dare to believe it is in all of us. It is submerged below the liquefied rock of hardship and dissension. Resiliency is shielded by the force field of denial and buried deep in the vault of fear. Most people when something becomes too hard they walk away or point the finger. I myself have come close a few times. For some they never had someone to go it with them. Recently someone very close to me said,

"Relationships are just too hard and not worth it."

Those words entered my ears and then bled directly into my broken heart because it sounded like the definition of what it means to give up. So how does one respond to that? I mean, that person was not wrong. The only explanation one could arrive at was that mistrust and internal injuries from eons passed had poisoned their future relationships.

Relationships along with life are difficult and always will be intricate and complicated as my Pastor even alluded to this past Sunday. There is when one thinks about it no way to respond because I imagine resiliency is detected through the actions of others and the environment we grow up in. To coin the phrase of some of the inner-city youth I worked with, *"I am a product of my environment"* they would say. Perhaps, it was broken relationships left unresolved with in the past of that loved one. This Author dares to imagine that while some individuals inspire the world through their words; it is through their actions they transform it.

I watched my mother even when she might not have known as she battled an abusive relationship and then my grandfather years later as he stood bravely against the cancer that had betrayed his body. He was like a strong oak tree slowly fading but only in body and not in spirit. At least not from where I stood. Though my Grandfather eventually lost that fight he won more than he will know as I grew closer to him in those final years of his life. Through the eyes of a teenager I witnessed a man once strong and full of spirit though his body was failing remain full hope and love even when the cards were stacked against him and his back was against the ropes. He won in another sense too and because of that I imagine "by grace" I will see him again when I close my eyes for the final time on this earth and open them for the first time again when I stand before Jesus Christ my lord and savior. I do not believe this; I know it to be certain, because *"faith is being sure of what we hope for and certain of what we do not see"* Hebrews 11:1. That I imagine is an absolute definition behind the modality that drives resiliency. Hebrew's 11:1 might well be its precise explanation for which there is no substitute. My mother taught me as Peter Kuzmic once said,

"hope is the ability to hear the music of the future and faith is the courage to dance to it today."

The Late 1980's

Stepping back in time for a moment or two, reminders of obscured anger and frustration waged war on the battlegrounds of my soul. For the longest time this Writer was filled with an anger that could not be explained and what light he had was obscured by shards of confusion and fears of tomorrow. The fear of who he would become when the roots from which he had sprung were so poisoned and laced with uncertainty. Like many of the youth I would one-day work with years later I acted out. My thoughts spoken through the microphone of misguided intention and exploits created in my life chapters once hard for me to reread.

Written on the discolored pages which first introduced me to elementary school is where I imagine a lot of the behavioral issues began. The biracial kid from the wrong side of the tracks always vandalizing school property, running from bullies and saying things I was never taught by my mother to say. While I never started physical altercations I somehow ended up in them. Once upon a time in the late 1980's I asked the question,

"Who would miss me if I were not here?"

I cannot remember the grade or exact year only that I was an elementary school kid wanting to disappear. By disappear I mean from existence. I even thought of jumping in front of a car once. It is crazy looking back now. In my first book of poetry I talked a lot about the Man in the Moon and how I wished he were real. I could see myself chasing him across the night sky hoping to hear stories of another time, only another childish escape from reality and planet earth.

Once upon a time I had this friend Laura who is no longer here in the physical sense of the phrase but forever in my heart. Often this Writer's thoughts are like a storm, unexpected as the memories of such times are placed on my computer screen. Even when out of order they seem to still come together and tether themselves intricately to the narrative I feel led to pen.

You see, when I was in grade school and getting into trouble while asking those crazy questions Laura would become an unexpected light in the darkness. She was a "Keeper of the Flame" one might say. Laura was a quite girl with long beautiful hair, a smile warm and eyes filled with a kindness rare these days. I still see her every time I talk to or see her twin sister Joanna whom I am still close to today. I was the renegade, the rebel, outsider, misfit, unpopular kid going nowhere, but Laura always spoke kindness and when I was excluded would include me with no hidden agenda or strings. Laura's positive attitude and genuine kindness was a lighthouse for the hopeless.

I will not relive how she died as it is not important, but rather I remember how she lived. We were friends until the day she died even though I had moved around a lot. I would see her when we had cross country meets and sometimes during other county events. It was in the year 2000 she left without warning and we had not yet graduated. The day I saw her face on the front of the newspaper announcing her death was the first time in my life I think I understood the emotions I felt. The harder to define feelings of sadness, loss, and yet, strangely hope danced on the ballroom floor of by heart. Had I not accepted Jesus Christ at a youth retreat a few years prior; that hope would not have comforted me. It was the hope of the "not gone forever" because I knew that regardless I would see my friend again because she loved Jesus Christ a savior I did not completely know yet!

Even upon visiting her mother in the weeks after she passed, she blessed me when her mom said,

"I found something you might want."

She went over to a drawer and pulled out and old envelope worn down by the years. Reaching inside of it she pulled out a faded piece of paper and handed it to me.

"What is it?" I asked.

"Just read it" Laura's mother said.

As I opened the folded paper I saw a familiar card from another time. When we were in grade school our teacher would have us fill out the "I saw Person's Name doing something nice" and on the card in my hand it read, *"I saw Clayton doing something nice."* Those who knew me would understand why this meant so much. To this day that thing she had seen remains a mystery. While I am certain Laura will likely resurface in future pages I will leave her here for a time. I know I traveled swiftly through twelve years of time and space but to tell this story I travel back through the portal of yesterday once more.

Living Here in Allentown

Imagine if you can emotions and feelings being placed on the dusty shelf of denial and left obscured beneath the Masquerade of one's so called individual autonomy that the world only sees the outside of. As you see that image illustrate a clear picture inside the walls of your individual mindscape, look close to those emotions left on that shelf and given free rein to boil over because the weight could no longer support the old wooden shelf they once sat on. That shelf is the very metaphor of one's soul. When this happens, and believe me because it was me, we are lead down a shadowy and desolate highway in which sometimes there is a point of no return. Lack of expression and understanding my own emotions would set me on such a road in which I would find myself in and out of different placements and group homes which were supposed to help individual's like me deal with anger.

When I still lived in Gettysburg in a time when Laura was still alive and I had not yet let go of the fantasies of hero's and demi Gods I was in and out of trouble so often. This Author was just an angry and frustrated grade school boy going through a rollercoaster of emotions. Occasionally, I would get beat up by the kids a grade ahead or called a racial slur. Often, the other children's words felt like shards of glass when they spoke and so a new war would begin. I would fight back against those who had done me no wrong and those I felt had. When I was not causing trouble in school I found an outlet through some of my neighbors. It is through the lenses of regret I find myself wishing I could just say,

"I apologize for how I treated you."

While I know I am not that kid I once was, I sometimes ask what really; was the catalyst behind the choices I made. Today I know pointing the finger of blame is an easy thing to do whereas taking accountability is much harder and a rarer attribute. In this area of my life and even in a current storm I am weathering this is a lifelong battle.

There was this neighbor who some might say today was the neighborhood busy body, a spinster or perhaps a loner. For my part I had done to her what the kids in school had been doing to me. I was no more than a miniature bully with curly hair and mischievous yet, unkind intentions. Sometimes when flashes pop into my head reminding me of those years this once foolish child wonder's, "what was Arnetta's story?" Perhaps we were more alike than I ever knew. I would later as an adult, cross paths with her again and to my surprise she forgave me. She once told me she never thought I was a bad kid. If some kid placed dog poop outside my sliding glass door or rang my door bell late at night I do not know what I would think especially had I stepped in that dog poop! These are only a few of my many escapades which came at the cost to others. Still these types of actions led me to different placement facilities.'

Upon being sent to these treatment facilities because of my anger and lack of a forgiving heart, it was the prayers of those who loved me that kept me going even if I did not realize it. They were sowing seeds and watering a potential flower growing in a concrete garden. I could not understand at the time that no one is perfect! If we were the world would be a dull place because there would be no creativity or originality.

I can still remember the silence of those facility hallways being interrupted by sniffling and tears. They were often lonely places where I felt like I would never overcome the situation I had placed myself in. Those nights were filled with shadows of a past I could not let go of. The dreams of my child hood ripped away by the wake of an abuser's storm seemed to throw me against the rocks of an uncertain future. The only comfort was when the cadence of a steady rain would fall because it masked the sound of my own tears which today I am no longer ashamed to admit I shed.

One facility stands out to me even though I cannot credit them for my transformation. Additionally; that metamorphosis was a slow hard process that even today continues with each breath I take. In a year I cannot recall I left my mother so that perhaps I would learn to talk rather than merely act out of impulse or anger. Perhaps, I would even learn to listen better. Over the years I have found that listening is still a battle I fight each day to become better at. It is in this arena I still fall at that Giant's feet often. There were individuals who would along with my mother teach me more about resiliency. It is for their privacy just as I did above with my neighbor that I have changed their names. The time they put into my life would help to one-day change how I lived and treated others.

So, it was I left the elementary school I spoke of briefly when I jumped ahead to highlight a synopsis of my friend Laura's touch on my life and headed to Allentown Pennsylvania just like the Billy Joel song.

Somewhere on Cedar Crest Boulevard my temporary home was a place called Wilson's Sanctuary. Upon my arrival I met with the intake worker and while I was outgoing and sociable, even likeable, I talked little about the root issues she likely was pushing for. My counselor I remember most. A tall thin woman maybe in her mid-twenties who I will call Kristine. She had long black hair that seemed to cascade down her back like a waterfall. Her voice was soft and kind. She was a very beautiful woman. Every evening we all had to sit in this circle and we would go around and tell the group aloud how we felt. If we had any issues that day the staff would focus on that. When the circle came around I was always the kid that would not hesitate to say *"pass."* At some point Kristine caught on rather quickly and would not allow me to say nothing. For the circle to keep moving I had to participate. I just said stuff so the other kids would not get mad at me for holding them up from their day.

I was one of the lucky ones I suppose because after some time there and I was there for two years, I could attend school off grounds. As I said being social and outgoing an extrovert was never an issue. Even today at age thirty-eight I can strike up a conversation with a stranger and do a public speaking event without preparing for it.

The facility sent me to an elementary school in Salisbury Township and like many things in my life I would mess that up too. Still while I was there I had a teacher who I heard recently passed away but not before we were able to reconnect after I had become a man over three decades later. We found each other via Facebook. Mrs. Shell was not just an amazing person who I quickly grew to love like a grandmother but the very definition of an extraordinary teacher. She would always say,

"Clayton, you are not a bad boy, I know you will grow up to be a wonderful man."

Honestly back then I did not believe her and even today who is good? We all are poisoned with sin. *"For it is by grace you have been saved, through faith--and this is not from yourselves, it is the gift of God."* - Ephesians 2:8. My fondest memory and one of the saddest was the day I was kicked out of the school for pulling the fire alarm. Before I did it, pulled the alarm that is, I heard that little voice whisper into an already overloaded mind;

"Don't mess a good thing up."

I did not listen and pulled it anyway but it was not so funny after. Especially when Mrs. Shell gave me a book on the Titanic because she knew even at that age I loved history. She was so good too at telling stories so much you thought you were in them. Who does that any more right? Looking at the book and then at me with eyes that revealed both disappointment and care she handed me that book hugged me and said,

"You will grow to be a wonderful man. Watch you will see."

I did not feel sorry as much for what I did. I felt like I let Mrs. Shell down, something I had been doing well to people who loved me for a while. It was the one thing I seemed so good at. In that moment a feeling I could not describe overtook me as I did not believe her words I would ever be a wonderful man. On what seemed like the longest ride back with Kristine because she did not say a word yet, only gave me that look through the rearview mirror my mother gave when I did something wrong; I opened the book to find Mrs. Shell's words etched again inside that book, and then signed *"Love Mrs. Shell."*

I Should Have Been Your Friend

When I returned home from Wilson's Sanctuary I went back to a new school in another town. I would discover that in all essence it did not differ from any other school. It's a funny thing really, as a child my mother once told me after I had threatened to runway,

"Clayton if you think the grass is greener in someone else's backyard, see if that is still true when you have to mow it."

I found that everywhere the road of life would take me there would always be individuals and circumstances that challenge us and force us to face them because one can only run for so long before he or she realizes regardless of where they run they must face reality. I thought I could go to this school and things and people would be different but they weren't and neither was I. It was in that middle school where perhaps my true biological roots began to grow in the Fields of Peer Pressure and the Lonely Meadows of Longing for Acceptance. That growth seemed to illustrate that I was "*The Kid from the Wrong Side of the Tracks*" poisoned with tainted DNA. However; because of decades now past, the "Rocky Mountains" along life's unpredictable road, and a newfound wisdom; it was my choices which confirmed that validity and not the origin or manner of my birth.

Slowly and without meaning to I became one of the same antagonists who once pushed me around and still did. As I walk through this unilluminated corridor in time and the words slowly appear on my computer; the black and white paintings on those dim lit walls of Yesterday tells a sad story about a friendship that should have and might have been. It still stings to share this moment in my history over two and half decades later and it had nothing to do with what others had done but what I had done to another. Furthermore; it is a chapter in a person's life they wish they could burn and rewrite. Yet; as this narrative has been outlining as clearly as it can regarding the past, what is written in the journal of yesteryear remains inscribed there until this mortal journey ends. The truth regardless of what some might say today, I was not the wonderful boy Mrs. Shell believed me to be even if I was a child. However, I know I must share this chapter of my life even if it hurts me to reread, heaven knows I must.

You see I would take my anger out on those who may not have necessary done me wrong much like Annette from earlier and a few others I will reference later. One individual stands out to me and his story I feel must be shared as he no longer walks this earth. Too often humanity which includes me, fails to see there are others in this world facing their own storms, their own trials and giants. For some, that circumstance they face is far worse than the one we may have faced.

Brett was a different, but by no means a bad person, quite the opposite. He wanted to belong like me. He was just trying to find his place in a world that did not seem to notice he was in it. I ask myself now that I am a man,

"What was so wrong with that?"

I, along with peers I wanted to like me, ridiculed him because he was a sixth grader that weighed over two hundred pounds, wore cowboy boots, a cowboy hat and jeans too tight to wear and a buckle to match the belt. I never physically hurt him but what I did was far worse and I have prayed that God will forgive me. I know he will but the hard part of forgiveness is one must forgive themselves. The battlefields of regret are brutal and I do not know if one ever really recovers from that.

The names I know from personal experience remain with you even after any physical damage that might have been caused has faded into shadow. The commentaries of the cruel and misguided, lower your ambitions, self-esteem, desires and it changes you.

This life has taught me often, that wounds to our flesh heal quickly, but words like knives cut deep and do not always heal. That saying we learned in elementary school "*sticks and stones may break my bones but names will never hurt me*" is a great big lie and a great deceiver! As I said earlier I never physically hurt Brett but I never stood up for him when the other kids would run up behind him and kick him, trip him and spit on him. I was no better than them and they never liked me anyway. They got a laugh only out of me mistreating another person. The laugh, the joke if you will, was me.

Years later I would discuss with my oldest son Isaiah about standing for something good. I shared Brett's story and my role as the villain in it. We were discussing forgiveness and bullying as he had come to an age of understanding where his daddy had come from and why I was always talking about the way we are to treat people. Soon after our conversation I wondered what had become of Brett. I never reconciled or thought of him until that day. However, what I would discover changed my life more than it already had after becoming a husband and a father and now I think of Brett often.

So, one day while looking through the phonebook I found his last name and saw it was still in the town we once lived; only his first name was not listed. The thing about small towns is no one ever seems to leave. Hesitant I picked up the phone and dialed the number. *One ring…. two rings…. three rings……*finally on the fourth a woman's voice said,

"Bieber residents"

In reply I said,

"Hello, I am trying to reach Brett we went to school together a long time ago."

I will never forget her words as long, as I live. She said,

"I am sorry Brett died he had a heart attack dear. Were you his friend?"

Pausing and pierced with guilt as those black and white pictures of a time not so long ago appeared on the canvas of my mind, I in a low tone voice said,

"No mamm."

In reply she responded with,

"Why are you calling then dear?"

Without thinking I said,

"I should have been his friend."

I told her of how I treated Brett and how I bullied him and ridiculed him, when I had been through the same thing. I explained to her about the discussion with my son and how after finding Christ years ago, joining the Army and working with troubled youth, that I was calling to tell Brett how sincerely sorry I was for the names, and the pain I caused him, because he unlike me he was a kind person. I was calling for forgiveness and the possibility to become the friends we might have been. When I write or do a public speaking engagement or even just revisit childhood briefly my mother always tells me I was just a kid and kids do mean things. They tell me regularly that I am too hard on myself. This I know to be true and maybe they are right. Maybe I was just a kid, but one thing I know now is I long for my boys to be better and stand up for those who might not be able to stand up for themselves. I should have been a voice speaking up from the crowd and the hand reaching out from Brett's personal darkness rather than an ax cutting a person down. Calling Brett's family was one of the hardest things I have ever done in my life. I thought she would just hang up, toss me aside, maybe blame me or curse me out but she didn't. She said instead,

"It must have taken courage to call and even more to tell me the truth. People change you know it is obvious from your call and I know that Brett would have forgiven you. No, he has I am sure of it."

Brett died in his late twenties and though his mother spoke kindness and compassion, demonstrated Grace and Mercy, I wonder would life be different had I been a friend instead of a bully. What if I would have stood up for him?

"*A few Good Men*"

As I mentioned earlier in the pages before these, my biological father remains to this day nameless and faceless behind that velvet veil of an obscured identity brought forth by days long past. For many years I lived without an earthly father to teach me what it was to be a man. No man of God to show me how to be brave when I was scared or how to remain humble and kind despite my circumstances. More significantly no one to teach me what it is that defines a man even if it was just accepting his faults.

When I look back upon my life I see the face of a man facing his own inward struggles but whom I recognize as my father all these years later. The man that taught me more about hope then anyone I would imagine. Hope of change, hope for something better than what yesterday's hand had dealt us. My dad taught me many lessons but one remains engraved in my mind and I see it as though it were yesterday even though it has been many years ago. I cannot recall for what I was being disciplined but I was perhaps fifteen or sixteen years old when I looked him in the eye and said,

"*I am not afraid of you, I have been pounded before. Besides you're not my real father.*"

Even as I type these words my skin cringes because of those awful words as I can still hear them in my head like it was yesterday. His response remains with me and will for as long as I live. As he took hold of me he looked me in the eye and said,

"I am not here to so you can fear me, I am here to teach you to be a man. One day you will understand that I am more of a father than you ever had because I am here."

He was and that side of him, the one that even when cut with foolish words of a teenage boy loved me enough to care. It was unconditional love.

It's been said that you will not be a good Father until you are a good Man. However, my father, my own life choices and my faith in God has brought me to question who is good? We are all flawed and tainted. My father though even with his flaws changed my life in ways he may never know. Now I said my dad taught me more about hope then anyone I know, but he also painted for me a beautiful mural of how God's touch on one's life changes a man. Through his example and personal growth, I witnessed the grace of God often. My father's nemesis like my own was once his anger. While he never once hurt me like I was so accustomed to before meeting him, his voice and language were his adversary. Yet, as the years have passed so quickly it seems, I watched a man struggling with anger, struggle with emotion just like me become a strong man of immense faith. Some might say, a real "Man of Steel" one of the "Few Good Men." You see Steel can melt but with God *"all things are possible."* People can claim to be good but it is only through Grace they are made pure.

My father taught me that a real dad regardless of if he is the one that helped bring you into the world wants to catch you before you fall, but instead, picks you up and brushes you off, and lets you try again. My father though I did not see it then was and is someone who wanted to keep me from making his mistakes but still let me find my own way, even when his heart broke in the silence of *"I tried to tell you"* each time his kids got hurt.

I have never told him just how important he has been to the evolution of my existence or the metamorphous of my ideals and values. Not too long ago I discovered that my father and I have much more in common than I ever thought. As I write these thoughts and they leave my mind and appear in front of me, I make a promise to God and myself. The next time I speak with my father I will tell him all I have chronicled here. I have tried every chance I get to tell him I love him and how blessed I am to call him my father. God sees beyond time, the past, the present, and the future while bringing into our lives individuals when we need them most to go the journey with us.

Dad if you are reading this I know there have been and may still be times when you have felt you were not a good father and your right you were not, you were and are a great father! I often feel like a failure next to you as I try to teach your grandsons that men are defined by actions and not the past. I try to teach them that real men like you keep pushing onward through the storm because they know that because of their faith the **Son** will shine with in them if they dare believe. I am blessed to have you in my life and I pray that I can be half the father, even a quarter of the man you are.

Shadows on the wall of Time

Everyone in their life one would think wants to be liked and fit in. It is part of our human nature and we were designed to be social beings. Middle school, now only shadows on the faded wall of Time brought forth the hesitation and fear that is the wintry forest of change. The lessons that came with pretending to be someone you're not out of such fear, or in my case lack of discernment often leads to not being accepted or liked. In that place one finds they are set up for a standard they can never reach and a price they will ultimately pay. I used to give my power of autonomy so often to someone else and exhausted myself in the process causing me to continually look outward instead of inward. I learned later in life that living without integrity is a key ingredient that will keep you trapped and living in the shadow of who you were meant to be. In the deep Vale of the human condition the resilient individual realizes that it is time to come out of the shadows and into the warmth of the sun.

Middle school was where I met my friend Sandy who even today so many years later is still one of my closest friends. She is as close to my heart as a sister and I love her as such. Much like Laura she had a kindness about her that was rare. Outgoing and charismatic she could influence a person to want to be better. Still even with her positive influence I made bad choices. The one positive difference though, I left the bully back in fifth or sixth grade never to be heard from again. This Writer learned that being a bully was not the way into someone's heart or to get them to like you. Sandy along with my English Teacher at the time helped me discover that I had a talent for writing. I remember writing this play that some of us would put on. Even though we never did, it was still nice to have such a friend willing to reveal that I had some other ability's I did not know I had. Often her just smiling at me or saying hello made a difference in my life.

Whenever I would get into trouble, be involved in food fights, pull the fire alarm again, even flood the third-floor bathroom, Sandy remained my friend. When I got older I tried to avoid the trouble makers, but looking back, often they need good friends the most. The outsider, the rebel, the misfit, the one deemed as difficult might believe they are worth more than those labels have indicated they are. Those shadows on the wall of time become the very moments that reminded them of the light in their lives. While I would be blessed with many light bearers like Sandy I considered that sometimes those shadows were the mirrors of the soul from which that light reflected off to change the trajectory of an individual's sense of value.

That persona which society has branded upon them because of unnatural social and moral selections should not be the scale on which they measure their own worth or value. I will always love my friend Sandy for never turning her back on me. She was the sister I needed in that time of my life. Throughout this weary traveler's life there have been people placed there as if the Universe was balancing out the adversities I had and would face with a brief reprieve. From the inner part of this Wordsmith's soul I now know that God controls the universe and that personal and spiritual growth does not differ from treasure hunting. In discovering purpose, meaning and self-worth, knowing you are loved no matter if your life is weather-stained with mistakes is priceless. Through this ongoing journey even when the boat in which I am rowing heads directly into the flood-tide of an unforgiving billow, the understanding that resiliency illustrates clearley that our whole lives are built around discovering who we are and what we believe.

There have been many individuals that have been like oxygen to my soul when it was dying to breathe and for that I now know I am forever blessed. Sandy if you are reading this along with others who know specifically who they are, thank you.

The Guidance Counselor

In some of my darkest moments, I was too afraid to face life alone even if I never would admit it. I needed the nonjudgmental ear of a friend who would listen and yet, dare to believe in what I could become. Someone to walk beside me as I slowly opened doors to my pain which led back through the doorway of days gone by. Sure, there was my mother and I had been to those group homes but sometimes one needs someone else and I never thought I would open those locked doors to a middle school guidance counselor. There had only been one before during my elementary school days named Joe. After all they are psychologist like the ones from the group homes and while I loved my mom, well...I do not know how to explain it I just connected with Mr. Wagner. He was different then the staff I had met in placement with maybe the exception to Ms. Shell and my individual councilor from my days in Allentown. Often, I opened my big mouth because I wanted to impress others so that perhaps I might find a way to love myself.

I could not find belonging as the Guardian within me was bound tightly to the chains of confusion and anger. I wanted to be liked. I mean, who doesn't right? All I longed for was to be loved. The yearning to heal even though I never came right out and said it was one of my deepest desires. Mr. Wagner along with others who later came into this Author's life taught me that while I used to think all that mattered in life was what people thought of my personality, my looks, or my ability's; that at the close of the day I only needed to take each day one at a time. Funny as I write this I know my mother told me the same thing often and now I tell my own kids that. The things that used to matter don't seem to matter as much anymore, and I now see life in a whole new way.

Mr. Wagner never once as I recall said the text books things like, *"how does that make you feel"* or *"why did you do this or that?"* He was more hands on and put me to work while we talked and he never said much or interrupted unless I tried to pull the wool over his eyes. He just seemed to know. Mr. Wagner would challenge me to what I might these days call "forward thinking" or "future pacing" and he might not realize that even though it was not until sometime later after I would make one of the worst decisions of my life I understood what those things meant. They were the gateways to the corridors of Introspection and the ability to see into the future based off a single choice. Not in the sense of being a Seer or fortune teller, but evaluating closer "cause and effect." Inside the glass halls of what one might call cathedral thinking, Mr. Wagner was cultivating a desire in me to set tangible goals that I would one day have learn to appreciate for the sake of an unknown future.

The thing I recall most looking back now is that Mr. Wagner had a gift for story-telling, it is how I suppose I even grasped on to this cause and effect thing and future pacing. As a Wordsmith myself I have cultivated through being a story-teller, that it is the yarns and hidden sorrows or dreams buried deep in the caverns of our soul that help immensely with this. This very narrative you are reading right now is my trying to sort out a way to illustrate what the "Spirit of Resiliency" is. By taking real moments and real people even if I have obscured their identities behind metaphorical illusions while placing them in to the Mindscape's of my readers so they can relate to various characters in a personal way.

I have found often in every story they come in the form of heroes trying to create change either in themselves or the world and villains trying to stop them. Those stories give our mind's a realistic pathway to understanding cause-and-effect. Even more so, when the time comes that the villain becomes a hero the Spirit of Resiliency is defined.

Attending that school was already hard as this Author was considered and still is by society a "minority." There were often moments I did not always say out loud what I was feeling when being bullied or facing a problem whether academic or social, but it was my middle school guidance counselor whom I now call friend all these years later who had a gift and ability to listen not just to words because life has taught me they are often deceiving; but rather through body language those unspoken words and attitudes.

Few people believed that perhaps I would grow into a "good man" if such men even exist. What I mean is how does one define good? Everyone might define it differently and so this Author means no disrespect he just knows because he is proof of how humanity is flawed. Maybe it is ok to say good or decent only God can answer I suppose. Even when the Chief of Police would not help me when some High schoolers would threaten me to the point of trying to run me over with their car and call me racial slurs while walking home from school or conducting my paper route; Mr. Wagner and two decent police officers both now retired believed in what I could become. That middle school guidance counselor though I would fall hard in my sixth or seventh grade year at the feet of my self-made giants always listened and never stopped believing. If he did he never showed it.

Inside the time capsule where I have stored these thoughts, the reason I grew to trust and admire Mr. Wagner was because of his innate ability to experience as one's own the feelings of others including me. Some might call that empathy or perhaps there were moments from his own youth in which he could relate, but I will on empathy. He had with in him a light I could not recognize back then. I only knew I enjoyed being its presence as it made even bad days bearable. His capability to identify why others did what they did and think the way they did took would one day teach me to future pace and evaluate closer the choices I would make. It would eventually be a fork in my past that would reveal how change was even possible and that it began with the way I thought about the world and essentially me.

The Science Teacher, Band Teacher and English Teacher

I imagine everyone can remember having a great teacher and the not so great teacher while they were in school. I came across three other types of adult influences while attending that middle school. The first would be the Science Teacher, the Second the Band Teacher and the third the English Teacher. All very different, all with their own lessons to teach me, but all had a profound impact on my life.

After growing close to Mr. Wagner, I had tried to become a better version of myself. It was so hard because I was always angry and did not know why. After all I had not earned a great name for myself as I was always visiting the in-school suspension teacher. Those days were no fun for sure. You sit there staring at the cracked and fading wall in front of you and for the entire school day you do only your school work. That wall often served for me as a reminder of where my life seemed to head. Right into a brick wall! Finishing early, I learned was not an option because the teacher would always find something extra.

To begin with those three other influences, this Author will start with the Science Teacher. I never did well in that class to begin with and I hardly ever understood what the man was talking about. My past mistakes like the fire, the fights, and the many days spent in, in-school suspension seemed to be the foundations for how he would profile me. Mr. Arne I know did not like me. Some might say,

"oh, that isn't true."

Yet, I know it to be. I remember sitting in his class and him asking us all a simple but complex question. It was not about photosynthesis or mitosis; it was not even about cell division or the periodic table, it was about the future. "Future pacing and cathedral thinking." In particularly It was a question I never thought about much. All I did know is I didn't want to be me. I did not want to be remembered as the fire starter, the instigator, the trouble maker. When the question came I said,

"I don't know" because I was afraid to answer. It was the truth too. I did not know.

Mr. Arne insisted that I answer or I would be sent to the principal's office for refusing to participate. It was not like I hadn't been there a million times before. One might say the principle had a seat with my name on it. I was not even being disrespectful. So, for probably one of the first times in my life I gave an honest answer. Looking at him with his expressionless face I proceeded with,

"Well maybe a probation officer or a youth counselor. I want to help others be better. I would like to be a writer maybe."

Bursting out in a chuckle he laughed and replied,

"Better pick something else because that idea is asinine. With your record it will never happen. Perhaps the writing thing but that is not a career."

I, taking offense to his tone sat up in my chair saying,

"I do not have a record!"

That was the same day and during that class I went to the bathroom clogged the toilets and flooded them for no apparent reason other than I wanted so badly to punch that man in the face. I know now that I am a man it would not have solved a thing but really would have served as validation of his claims. The Dean of Assistant Principle could be heard over the loud speaker instructing no one to leave the third floor because water had run down to the first floor and out the light fixtures of one of the fifth-grade rooms. Yes, this was more than one day of in-school suspension it was five!

Sometimes I wish I would run into The Science Teacher like I did the Police Chief many years later. When I worked at the County Court House as a Security Officer, the Chief of that town I once lived in, the same man who when my mother told him about people trying to run me over and calling me racial slurs just responded with,

"well this is primarily a white community."

I will never forget when he said to my boss at the courthouse,

"you gave him a gun?"

I wish for this not to boast or brag but for him to see with his own eyes how wrong he was. I had done by God's Grace everything I said I would that day in class. I joined the Army believing the commercials about "being all I could be", became a clinical counselor, a youth development Aide Supervisor working with the roughest and most dangerous young people in the State of Pennsylvania. I even became a State Food Inspector which was as close to law enforcement I would come and it is my occupation. The grip of Grace has blessed me with the chance to speak to groups of people and become a writer of such things.

Once a troubled student I learned from the Science Teacher and the Police Chief that in this life people will judge us for our sins. They will often try to remind us of what we once did. However, they may judge our earthly existences' but they have no power over our soul. As the Dragon Bruce Lee once said, I learned that, "*I am not in this world to live up to their expectations, and they are not in this one to live up to mine.*"

Now the Band Teacher he was different. My love for music and now creative writing for a while helped to prevent those visits to in-school and my special seat in the Principal's office. Mr. Wareham was a man with a love of music. He could see in each student the ability to express themselves and in a few others the ability to inspire. Almost like the Horse Whisperer he could speak when others had tried but could not. I looked forward to what we called sectionals where the instrument you played had their group lesson. I tried hard to stay out of trouble just so I would make it to band class and jazz band. Since I struggled to read music and played mostly by ear, Mr. Wareham while wanting me to learn how to count my measures and become more effective at timing taught me the art of improvisation. Like life, improvisation I believe is that ability to hear the music no one else can hear. It is inside of your mind's eye and cannot be stolen from you because it is your creation. Hidden melodies that can only be heard in the musicians own soundscape and then set free into the real world through song.

Only God, can look deep into your soul and see what you see. On that same note, see what I did there? God sees that which we do not. It is the extensions of emotions which require different choices to be made, and sometimes you make them without thinking because you have faith that the notes and the song will make sense even if it is only to you. Life is the same way. When we wonder, *"what do I want to do, who do I want to be?"* When faced with impossible choices and yet we make the hard one because we have faith that God will help us make sense of 'Life's" ever changing song, we demonstrate the Spirit of Resiliency in its purest form.

Even with all my failures, The Band Teacher saw more than the music inside of me. He saw a possible future and that is why he was hard on me. Whether it was because I did not practice or because I was struggling in other classes he did so to remind me it is those who care about us who must tell us what we need to hear and not what we want to hear.

The Guardian of the Ashes remains bound to the past because they do not want to hear what they need to hear. More important they do not have individual's like the few friends, a mother who chose me, a father who would one day love me, a Band Teacher or as I will be mentioning next an English Teacher to support them, even when they have crashed and burned. If I could say one thing to Mr. Wareham, it would be that he helped me to believe that I could become *"a music maker and dreamer of dreams."*

Despite the lows, this Wordsmith enjoys writing his thoughts and memories, even hopes and dreams because sometimes they manifest into vivid paintings that bring those moments to life with color. The black and white seems to jump from the pages fashioning sketches that only I could see, feel and hear, even the ones that hurt to recall. In addition, those moments are mine alone. This Author owns them regardless of what they might have made him feel. My middle school English teacher Mrs. Schultz reinforced that gift by helping me to find love in poetry beyond just reading rhymes but in analyzing them. What did they mean? What was the poet trying to say? What did Frost mean when he penned,

"I have promises to keep and miles to go before I sleep?"

Mrs. Schultz once told me if I write from my heart, that if I were to describe a rainbow to a blind man they would see every color bright and it would illuminate brilliantly in their mind's eye. In other wards those moments, those hopes, sorrows and dreams would become real to the reader. It was a way for me to finally express what was going on in the world I called my life even if I did not clearly understand it. She may not have known it back then but Mrs. Schultz helped shape the future of a struggling kid drowning in the oceans of past through writing.

As I look back on my middle school years which were significant to the path I traveled and would travel; the three teachers touch on my life illustrate how positive or negative influences from a teacher early in life can have a great effect on the life of a child. I think about the Science teacher and wonder if he ever realized the way he came across or how his words did not differ from the day I got that scar on my left hand. Maybe he never knew and perhaps as a student I could have been a better version of myself than what I was.

"Stain Glass Masquerade"

Anger's tremendous energy has a powerful kinesthetic element to it. For some of us, it is necessary to vent our anger, to scream at a wall absent from others or punch a pillow. I would later in life embrace Taekwondo and Muay Tai Kickboxing as an outlet. While for others anger can be processed in a quieter, less physical way, perhaps using meditation or mindful strategies to help us release it which do not contradict our core values. Still, the best meditation for me has been prayer. I have found that anger and frustration beyond what is normal often masquerades under the veil of various other, more discreet and obscured labels such as "irritation," "impatience" and "troubled" all labels I was connected to. Holding onto that bitterness for too long fills us with antipathy and that sullenness is poisonous. It is like venom from the fangs of the snake which paralyzes and traps us, keeping us bound as Guardians of the Ashes. This Writer would discover from a choice he would make which would alter the course of his existence; that so often it hurts us far more than it hurts those who have hurt us.

Once upon a time, I used to think; all that mattered most in life was what people thought of my personality and ability's. All I wanted was to change the way others saw me and just maybe if I was a hero, the good guy for once…. well than everything would be better. Still no matter how much I wanted to fit in I never would. At least, not back then.

Plans were set in to motion in my mind when I saw an open shed on my way to school. I went into it without thought of consequence. Beneath a wooden tool table in a five-gallon gas can was my so-called solution. Pouring the accelerant anywhere and everywhere I could I set the shed ablaze. Making my way to the crossing guard I reported seeing a fire, the one I myself was responsible for. What I didn't know because impulsiveness drowned out rationality was there was an apartment above it. While no one was in it or harmed the sinister whispers of "*what if*" haunted me for some time after I had been discovered to be the perpetrator of such a horrible deed. That action eventually placed me on juvenile probation. That was the intersection where lost and found collided head on.

There at that cross roads of my youth I realized that I was blaming all the wrong people for my actions. While I believe some of our ability to deal with hardships and failure can be attributed to biological traits and genetics, it has a lot more to do with the environment and people around us. Our parents, siblings, peers, educators, and community all play a vital role in shaping who we become. As the stain glass masquerade of placing all of that on those "vital" environmental and social variables in the equation of life there is one absolute. "Choice". Regardless of our history each person chooses who they will become. Life is tough and we all have our own challenges to face. We need not face them alone. With a caring heart and encouraging hand, we can all play a role in supporting others through their greatest hardships. However, we cannot do that until we heal ourselves and we cannot heal ourselves until we renew our mind. Only then can we break the chains.

Breaking the Chains

It is not the easiest thing to do, but letting go of the past may be one of the wisest things we can do in the entirety of our life time. I know for me it has probably saved my life but more important my soul. I now no longer wrestle with the reason of not so much letting go as moving forward. Can one even move forward without remembering what it was that brought them to the place where they are? I do not believe so but this Author has been wrong often in his life.

I have been brought to the newfound belief I am worth more than my past no matter what others might think. Until I could open my eyes and believe I could change my story and rewrite it, all these aspects of my life which I have been sharing would not be altered. For far too long I was telling myself that I was not good enough and that's what I saw all around me and believed it to be absolute.

In a summer I cannot recall the chains which weighed me down would be broken and left behind me in the sands of yesterday while at a youth retreat. This speaker talked of a man named Jesus, but he was not just any man. I had been to church because mom made us go. I remember all the stories from Sunday school. Yet, this was different. The man spoke of Jesus's Father and that he was God himself a creator full of grace and mercy. At first it was like most stories, hard to believe or imagine.

I listened not thinking anything would come of it but what the speaker was saying as the moments went on, was almost as if he were speaking directly to me. As I looked around there were hundreds of other teens which made it surreal because my whole life story was being read back to me through the words of a man I never met. For the first time I sincerely felt as though just maybe this Jesus was the real deal. There at the center of the mind's eye I imagined perhaps, when Jesus looked at my life he saw potential; he saw a miracle I never could. Like a breath of fresh air my mind cleared and my life could be observed objectively through the Grace of God and the interceding unconditional love of Jesus. The truth I was loved even If I had not loved myself became a catalyst for new hope. Additionally; while my purpose was and is still unknown, I had one as does every person. It was that summer I accepted Jesus Christ into my heart. The road since has still been rough and while my storms of yesterday are not my storms of today I know I do not face them alone. Sometimes if I am being transparent, the storms of today rage harder than those of yesterday. The chains of my past were broken because of faith, hope and the greatest of the three, love. Each day seems to be a new battlefield but the faith that Christ is in me is as solid as the ground I stand on.

"It is always important to know when something has reached its end. Closing circles, shutting doors, finishing chapters, it doesn't matter what we call it; what matters is to leave in the past those moments in life that are over."

— Paulo Coelho,

The Boy Who Left Home

G.K Chesterton once said, as I would later be reminded by my Senior Drill Instructor,

"The true soldier fights not because he hates what is in front of him, but because he loves what is behind him."

Chesterton's words have always been inspiring to me even though at first that is not why I would join the military. I was no hero nor did I want to risk my life for a cause. I loved my country sure……but did I want to die for it? Not really. I left because I loved little not even myself. The only people I loved was my mom and dad. I joined because the naïve teenager of my youth thought if he put on that uniform perhaps all those people he wanted to be liked by, all those people who only saw a troubled youth would change. I joined the Pennsylvania Army National Guard 108th Field Artillery when as a junior in High School. My ideals and reasoning were jaded and no different from the early years of my life when I escaped into the stories of God's and Demi God's. In that summer of 1999 I would learn more about being a man, then I ever would about becoming a soldier.

My recruiter was a smooth talker with his own agenda but I had mine too. The Sergeant First Class was a tall thin man with blue glassy eyes. His uniform neatly pressed and dress shoes shined. The medals and ribbons on his chest told the story of one who had served for a long time though I did not know what any of them meant. I saw at first a man I wanted to be like because of the outward appearance. He looked like someone from a movie or out of the pages of history. I would discover that sometimes the rugged and worn down, the misunderstood, the misjudged or stereotyped individuals have more integrity and honor than individuals who dress, talk, and fit the mold of society.

Like many young people I did not look at the contract I was signing and that summer I would do whatever it took to get in and leave my small Mayberry like town behind. Since I had been an infant if you recall from earlier pages I was dropped on my head and my hearing was fading with each year. My recruiter knew this as well and because a recruiter's advancement with in the military depended on if he met his enlistment quota, he would help me cheat the hearing exam.

"They always test the right ear first" he said with a smile. *"So, when the right ear is done just turn the headset around so that you will hear the left in your right"* he concluded.

Though I had given my life to Christ a few years before; the temptation became sin as I went through with it knowing I would not be caught because the audiologist put me in a booth with no windows. They did not actually watch the soldiers while the hearing exam was being administered. There was no surprise when both ears passed with one hundred percent hearing. Little did I know in that summer of 1999 God would put me on a collision course with resilient men and women that would change the way I saw the world and myself. They were true individuals of integrity, initiative and honor. There was nothing special about the way they dressed or where they were from but there was something special and extraordinary about them.

The program I enlisted into was called a "split option." This is when a soldier leaves home for basic training and upon his or her return they must graduate High School or obtain their GED. Once completed the future soldier would leave again for AIT or commonly known as A School where they learn the job they chose. While my peers were enjoying a summer filled with parties, swimming and vacations, my plane left Dulles International Airport in Harrisburg Pennsylvania and touched down a few hours later in Richmond Virginia where I was shuttled to Fort Jackson South Carolina. I watched out the window of that shuttle as an open road was all that could be seen. Where the sky and land met I could not tell as the sun retreated beneath the veil of the western sky. Moments in time, brief ones entered my mind and the story of where I had come from and my false sense of why I joined played like an "I love Lucy Rerun" on the movie reels of my memories The feelings of regret for how I had left home haunted me whispering and laughing in my mind's eye as my mother and I were not seeing eye to eye and I had been the fool not her.

My shuttle arrived at the Reception Battalion where a tall African American man directed us in a loud thunderous voice to get off the bus. It was only with in the first few minutes I questioned my choice to leave home. As I said I knew in my heart of hearts I was no hero. This earthly vessel was not built to soldier whether domestically or in some distant foreign land. That first night The Senior Drill instructor made all recruits stand at the position of attention for approximately four hours though it seemed much longer. Drill Sergeant Tate while a hard man was what I would discover one of the "Few Good Men" with character made of a rigid and steadfast Steel able to withstand anything. As the weeks progressed I learned how to fire a rifle, call cadence, perform drill and ceremony and much more, but none of that as important as integrity, honesty and honor. That summer molded me in ways I never thought it would.

All around me were young men and women of all backgrounds, beliefs, values, religions, ethnicities and walks of life. Some of them even from other parts of the world trying to escape their third world country for a better life and the only common ground we had was the color of our uniform and our new first name, "Private." Each young man and woman were there for their own reasons that only the individual could attest to. Senior Drill Instructor Tate's official welcome will forever remain with me as he was open and candid about what lied ahead.

"This road, this choice you have made to wear this uniform and leave home you will find will not be what you expected or imagined. During the next few weeks you will discover who you really are and you might not like what you discover, in fact it might even trouble you. It may just be the most important discovery of your life because until we know who we are we will never know who we are meant to be."

Just like that the intro was over. It was not very inspirational in that moment if you ask me. Except for maybe the last three lines because honestly, I was just some kid from nowhere Pennsylvania and did not know who I was.

When I first met Private Rivera, I was a naive and chauvinistic individual without even realizing or intending to be. Michelle Rivera was from Aspen Colorado and dreamed of jumping out of planes. This was the first year that basic training was coed and the bond we would form changed the way I saw others too. Michelle was a little bit taller than me and she had this certain energy about her. Her long black silk hair came to the middle of her back and she had emerald green eyes. She smiled little but looking back now none us did. On the firing range she was untouchable and a force to be reckoned with, on the physical fitness field stronger than all the women and second only to one male. No, it was not me. I never foresaw us becoming friends but we did. During that summer my path intersected with another Drill instructor facing his own demons. One of them being the venomous viper of alcoholism and the other more formidable Nemesis, anger. The two are never a good combination.

Basic training is two weeks of reception and nine weeks of actual basic training. Somewhere in the middle while preparing to complete an obstacle course Drill Sergeant Morningstar told each of us while in formation whoever completed the course first would be rewarded with a steak dinner and a Friday of no duty or training. Like Ashton Kutcher in the film "The Guardian" I was about setting those records and being first. I might not have been able to not out PT everyone else but I could tear that course up. So, we were off! Where my speed came from I do not know. When I look back perhaps it was me running from yesterday trying to be a better version of my former self or just attempts to prove to myself that I could succeed subconsciously.

The course was much like a mini Spartan race or mud run because it had rained the night before as I crawled through that mud and under barbwire. The wall following the long crawl was maybe five feet up and at its base on the other side a large pond filled with stagnant pond like water waited. I charged through that course like a soldier storming the beaches of Normandy during WWI and it felt good.

Deeper into the woods a large set of monkey bars which crossed a river of mud signaled the half way mark. Looking back, I saw no one behind me. As the saying goes it was in the bag so to speak. In those days arrogance convinced me I was built like a 1967 Charcoal GTO, American Muscle low to the ground but built to Last. A few feet beyond the river of mud was a one-hundred-pound dummy that needed carried up a hill maybe half a mile long give or take. This was probably the hardest part as I dragged GI Bob up that knoll to carry him to safety.

More turns and small hills revealed themselves beneath the veil of the forest trees canopy as long branches reaching into the path made way to slow runners down. There was about four-hundred meters; the length of one lap around a high school track where the path was so narrow and the hidden pot holes and roots became potential ankle breakers. As I came to the end of the course a tall wall maybe twelve feet with a rope descending to climb up and over, now stood between me and my steak dinner. That place and time found only in my mindscape where the world seemed stopped was not so strange, but the vertigo of the conscience was overwhelming. This soldier could not decide if he should jump on the other side of the wall or if there was something he had been missing. Dare I say, this Soldier jumped foolishly, where Drill Sergeant Morning Star and Senior Drill instructor Tate stood waiting.

"I did it drill sergeant easy no sweat" I said out of breath while trying to obscure that I was exhausted….

"Where is your squad private?" Drill sergeant Morningstar said with disapproval in his voice and yet; surprisingly sober.

Senior Drill Instructor Tate pulled me aside looked me in the eye and said something I will never forget. I had over the weeks come to admire the man and respect him greatly. He even took me to his church off base once. So, when he spoke I listened.

"Private, on the battlefield whether in some other country or in life it does not matter how fast or strong you are if you go it alone. Leaders, which I believe you can be fight not because they hate what is in front of them but because they love what is behind them. The measure of a man is not defined by where he comes from but by the choices he makes, the people he inspires through that leadership. Real Leaders, good men lead from the back not the front."

I knew in that moment I failed because for much of my life I made it all about me. That vertigo of the conscience was trying to tell me as much and I like those "do not dive in the shallow end of the pool" warnings ignored it and I jumped into the ocean of "self" where I nearly drowned.

So now knowing about this event I can speak more about Michelle's resilient spirit and how I came to admire her. During training she had sustained a stress fracture in he left foot and the fear of being recycled which meant basic training all over again whispered the possibility into her mind. On top of that not many females were signed up to attend Airborne School and the military was her escape from an abusive home life, so failure could not be an option. Before graduation we had to qualify on the shooting range, complete our final physical fitness exam and endure a four-day exhibition covering twenty miles in which everything we had learned was applied in the field. The range was no problem for her she was one of three to shoot Hawkeye which is a perfect score. The run however took its toll and I found myself running beside her, pushing her and calling cadence, reminding her she was an American Soldier but more important my friend. She completed her run with in the time she needed.

It was during the exhibition march this once American Soldier discovered who he was and wanted to be as that first day intro Senior Drill Instructor Tate gave echoed through his mind through the soundscapes of inspiration. As we marched beneath the heat of an unforgiving Sun; the sweat pouring into our eyes burned from the salt hidden in it and blurred our vision. In our hands we held our rifles while upon our backs we carried a thirty-pound rucksack as each mile seemed to drag. There were no conversations except the ones we had in our own minds to keep us going or the occasional halt or drink water command given by a drill instructor. The three nights beneath the stars were a relief but sleep remained hidden from many of us. Two of those nights were muggy and the mosquitos and other biters of the night left their marks on our skin.

It was the final day of the expedition march and the heat was unbearable. With maybe three miles to go I looked to see my friend and fellow soldier Michelle fall to the ground. The weight on her foot proved too much and she could go no further. If she did not finish she would be recycled and I promised I would tell no one about her foot and so I did not. I would not stand back and watch her be recycled. She worked too hard. For the first time without thinking about why, I grabbed her rucksack which was only a bit lighter than my own and placed it on the front of my body. The only thing we could not touch was another soldier's rifle which I could not have carried anyway.

"*What are you doing?*" she said.

"*I am not finishing this without you! You will be Airborne even if I do think it's crazy to jump out of a perfectly fine plane*" I said with a smile.

I will never forget the way she looked at me. She did not need to say anything and I knew we would always be friends no matter where the future would take us or how many miles away from one another we would be. Drill Instructor Morningstar in a loud voice and slurred speech yelled,

"*leave that ruck pri, pri…. private and her*" he seemed to stutter before finishing the sentence.

That first week of basic I probably would have. Yet; something in me changed that I could not explain.

"*I cannot do that Drill Sergeant.*" Only my words were not said in a disrespectful tone like I would have weeks before either.

Then again, I would not have bothered to say anything weeks before. Drill Instructor Morningstar stopped the formation looked at me and said,

"leave her, obviously she was not meant to be a soldier in my Army" he stammered as even his peers observed the interaction with looks of disappointment in their eyes.

Finding my voice, I calmly said,

"not more than two weeks ago drill sergeant you asked me where my squad was because I finished the obstacle course without them. Private Rivera is my squad mate and fellow soldier as is every person here marching beneath this unforgiving sun. I mean no disrespect but I am not finishing this without her or anyone else here for that matter."

You know that "oh crap" moment that comes into your mind when you think maybe I should not have said that, but then you realize oh crap I just did? Yep that is the "oh crap moment." I could see it oh to clear but the words had been uttered from my lips. I imagine throughout my life I have been there done that and have earned the T-Shirt more than once. I was thinking, where that came from because I knew I was in trouble.

"Ok private" drill instructor Morningstar said, *"we will see how you feel about being a hero when we get back to the unit and we have you participate in some extracurricular activities."*

What had I done? I looked over to where Senior Drill Instructor Tate was hoping he would intervene but I saw something I had not seen the whole time I was there. He smiled slightly at me as if to say, *"I told you so."* It was a nonverbal acknowledgement I finally had done the right thing despite the consequences. It might have been the first time in my entire life.

When we returned Drill instructor Morningstar instructed everyone but me to sit down and take a load off. Looking at me he said,

"alright hero pushup position, rifle over your hands and do not remove the rucksack on your back."

My arms burned, and my spirit was fading. Why didn't Senior Drill Instructor Tate step in I asked myself? As the sweat dripped from my uniform and my brow I saw in my mind's eyes the last twelve weeks and the journey I had been on.

"I will break you private……. I will so help me God!" Morningstar screamed in a now hoarse voice.

My thoughts were *"God please do not help him help me."* He was right you know I was at that verge where everything I had done was about to unravel because I wanted to get up and punch him in the face. There at the edge of my world's mindscape I stared into the abyss of defeat. In that moment before plunging off the edge I looked up see my friend Michelle place herself in the push up position, rucksack on her back rifle over her hands and sweat in her eyes. One by one my peers joined in until all of thirty of us were in unison.

I did not understand that Senior Drill Instructor Tate had not intervened earlier because he was teaching me one last lesson. He was teaching us all a lesson. He was culturing in us that as I may have said earlier, some individuals inspire the world through their words, but through their actions they can transform it. I was not changing the world I know, but I discovered that when it is not all about me my own life changes, I changed and for once it felt good.

I tried to hide my tears and camouflage it with the sweat so my battle buddies would not see that what they had done as they gave me the last ounce of endurance to not give up and it was in that moment Senior Drill Instructor Tate in a firm voice said,

"Enough! Everyone return to your dorms, shower and get a good night sleep. In two days you graduate."

On graduation day all the drill instructors were there except Drill instructor Morningstar. Senior Drill instructor Tate shook my hand congratulating me for making it through basic training as he gave me one last smile. I never saw him again. However, that smile spoke louder than any words ever could. Resiliency is defined by the character of a person and both Michelle and Senior Drill Instructor Tate were two of the most resilient people I ever knew. While they will never know I am talking about them because I have changed the names in this section and they could be anywhere or nowhere in the world; I have thought of them often as I remember the summer I left home a boy and would return a man.

Introspection from of a Soldier Returned

Before first leaving home, I used to observe people on the streets of my Mayberry like town and in my High School and assume that their animated and lively conversations/ interactions teamed with a sense of security because of their gifts and talents were evidence they lived a life much better than mine.

In another time this Author recalls sitting on that stage at his high school graduation trying to imagine what it would be like to be someone else, anyone but me. I knew I was leaving for the military but also the reality I was no hero still stood laughing in the back of my mind. The future was so uncertain back then and at times even today still is. My twelfth-grade year I felt as if life was stacked against me and that the weight of those unknown tomorrows rest on already weary shoulders. Still, upon my return home as I prepared for the world I not only learned that summer about integrity but my return would teach me I cannot change other people; I can only reinvent myself. To do so though; I had to change the way a thought about things because those thoughts dictated my actions.

In the spirit of honesty there are still many days when I can feel the energy of my existence being sucked right out of me. Like the house torn from the Midwest during a violent tornado, this Writer has felt even after moving forward from the past; as though he was being thrown, beaten and battered by the trials of this undefined and unpredictable life. As a matter of fact, even as I have typed these words and expressions of hope and love; I have myself have been struggling with depression and unexplainable feelings. However, I am not alone on that battlefield because Jesus Christ is with me! A newly fashioned mindset reveals I have been blessed and given all I will ever need in this life even when it they cannot be seen. This narrative's main hub is about that very truth. The initial source of this anxiety I cannot find and so I turn to God for help. For no reason to think of sometimes I want to cry or sleep. Regardless, I will fight it like every battle before me.

The journey I have been on, even the moment's which appear smaller than others in this narrative reveal yet another collective truth as to if a person will remain a "Guardian of the Ashes or become a "Keeper of the Flames." Like this Author has mentioned before, we must change the way we think to change the way we live and that is a choice! Therefore, rather than continue down a path of self-destruction or drowning in the oceans of the past one must choose to move forward even if it hurts. For me, most of my life I was slowly allowing the world and the past to consume the borrowed time, hopes, dreams and energy we all live on.

This Author came home to find all the people he wanted to be like were doing all the same things and living the same lives. The town did not change but I discovered I had. I even discovered I was slower to anger and had more empathy for those around me. As with my commitment to becoming a Christian, that summer away from home at Fort Jackson allowed me to introspect myself in those subterranean coves of my soul where no other man or woman could see and the only other being that could; was God himself.

It was an inspection of my thoughts and values evaluated from a Christian perspective. Through that process the Spirit of Resiliency allows one to embrace change as it is so many things woven into a big quilt of possibility. It's spine-chilling, electrifying, and unpredictable, but most of all it is essential to moving forward from that which held us prisoner to yesterday.

After the return home there were time when I passed people in town whether running cross country or even in the surrounding area, I realized I did not want to be them. Though I still had not discovered my own autonomy in the grand spectrum of things, I did discern I wanted to be my own man.

Cadences of Change

In late June of 2000 just a few weeks after my friend Laura had been killed in the car accident I mentioned earlier, I walked across the stage of my high school to receive my diploma, something I once thought I might never see or hold. During my last year of Highschool the winds of change I knew were blowing and as I briefly mention earlier I was scared. There was no more time really to live care free. Yet, this summer would differ from the last. My mission to continue discovering who I wanted to be and the opinions of others no longer seemed to matter much unless there was what appeared to be sound reasoning.

Now on another plane headed for Fort Sil Oklahoma almost fourteen hundred miles from home a new chapter was being penned. That plane ride gave me time to reflect as new-found observations without negative judgment was the drumline where the cadences of change beat steadiest upon the diamond plated snare drums of a life in forward motion. I was determined to take the life experiences, the heartache, the loss, the pain and the hope from my life and use it when I needed it the most to become a better person than I was the day before.

It was over Nashville, Tennessee 30,000 plus feet in the air I concluded this. To truly change as a person in a positive way; I not only needed a more profound insight into the reflecting lakes of Time which held my thoughts, past, present and future; but rather I needed to submit to God everything. I had to ask Him for the ability to observe my own decisions and outcomes through the same lenses He sees me with and without the judgment of a world view.

The Cadences of Change I have also found are not always so steadfast and positive, change never is. However; "Stepping out of the Ashes" takes courage and with courage there is often a fear of what will be lost. This moment in my life several thousand feet in the air it dawned on me just as the Sun rises each morning in the Eastern Sky. My main struggle all my life besides not moving forward from the past was not living my life with purpose or drive because I did not know what it was. There were many times in my life even after accepting Jesus Christ where I was not being true to myself or my values. I do not mean as the world has illustrated in magazines or on television.

For the first time on that long flight I think I faced my fears and building empowering beliefs that serve others in the same light that Jesus Christ came to Serve and witness. I had not fully changed because truthfully even though my mindset was improving I was still not living up to my fullest potential. The same might be said of me today. There was no real excitement tugging at me to get out of bed each morning and be the man God desired and fashioned me to be.

This Author, like many thought all the struggles and hardships he faced was God trying to teach him something when it was never about Clayton. Sure, I know he loves us all. Yet, God made none of those bad things happen that was life! That idea was selfishness weaved into the blanket of self-justification and purpose. So, it is that I have come to a steadfast truth. Those times that have tried our soul, those moments that nearly broke us become stories for others to find hope in. How we have come through it is where the lesson is learned and where the Spirit of Resiliency flourishes. The lesson learned is really one and one only, "*I can do all things through Christ who strengths me*" as I have stated often before. However; for that to be true I must change the way I see the world and those in it and how I see myself.

As my plane touch down in Oklahoma it was evident to me that God and I were having a telepathic conversation in which he was convicting my heart to march with and not against the Cadence's of Change. I felt that summer evening God's presence and realized that even though change required a lot of me and my willingness to trust Him he was not telling me to always agree with the world and those in it only to see them through eyes of Grace and Mercy. He wanted me to see myself through those same two lenses.

Full Bird Colonel

Fort Sill Oklahoma 1,400 miles from home greeted me with the familiarity of military life as the cadences and yelling of the Drill Instructors could be heard echoing through the reception battalion and it reminded me of what I had experienced that summer before in Fort Jackson South Carolina. Along with others who had completed basic training we waited to begin our school of specialty. For me back in those days before technology kind of made it obsolete much like an eight-track cassette tape, I was to be a surveyor. GPS and computer technology has since replaced the azimuth I was going to learn to use. This now relic of an instrument did not differ from a compass the military utilized to create an observation using an azimuth and distance. The exciting thing is that since there are many different types of surveying the field artillery surveyor/meteorological crewmember monitored weather conditions so the field artillery team could fire and launch missiles accurately. Their role was and is for those units who still utilize the traditional surveyor crucial in the support of infantry and tank units during combat.

Now because communication was crucial and my hearing was failing I knew that I could not in good conscience continue with the masquerade I had allowed myself to be privy to the summer before. For if that day came that I would find myself in some distant land and lives depended on if I heard my battle buddies accurately haunted me and so I confessed.

I was brought before the Commanding Officer at time, a full Bird Colonel. There I stood in front of an African American Woman perhaps in her mid-sixties maybe standing at five feet. Her face worn down not by age but rather it seemed more like one who lived through the storm and had seen both the best and worst of humanity. I did not realize how right I was. This Narrative has been focused on many things and resiliency being the main hub in which all other memories and moments in time have been penned and converge on one another. Never had I met an individual like the Colonel.

"You realize you are subject to court martial private of fraudulent enlistment" she said a stern voice.

"Yes ma 'mm" I replied with a slight tremble in my voice and a lump in my throat that was growing with each second that passed.

Looking me directly in the eye she said,

 "Someone helped you do this, to cheat the first exam, if you tell me I will not hold you responsible as you have come to me now with this."

Deep down I was ready to blurt out my recruiter's name but the lessons of responsibility from the year before seemed to resonate with in me and instead I said,

"ma 'mm I am responsible, I knew it was wrong but chose to do it and compromised who I was, my values, my ideals so I accept this choice and own it."

In a perhaps less stern tone she asked,

"Why?"

Not thinking I responded with,

"ma 'mm I come from a small town where most people there only know me as the bad kid, the child left to die at age five and placed into foster care. I wanted so bad to start over. I thought if I could wear this uniform people would look at me differently. It is only because of last summer at basic training and all I learned about doing the right thing even when it hurts that I came forward today. You do not know ma 'mm what it is like to feel like an outsider and want to matter."

For as long as I live; I will never forget her words as the echo through the crystal caverns of my memories. Nor will I ever again assume to know anything regarding the feelings or life of another. As a look of calm came over her face she said,

"Private I am an African American Woman and a Colonel in the United States Army. I grew up in Birmingham Alabama during the Civil Rights Movement and marched with my momma and granddaddy along with Dr. King, so I do know what it feels like to be the outsider. We Prayed for equality and peace, we had faith in the God who created us that one day as Dr. King said we would not be judged by the color of our skin but by the context of out character. Character private is what people will see. That is what they will remember"

She not only had to transcend the color barrier of her generation but also the gender barrier and I there on that hot summer day was painted a beautiful picture of what the Spirit of Resiliency looked like from that Colonel whose Grace allowed me to choose another occupation or accept a medical discharge. I chose another occupation.

In this Author's last manuscript, I talked about success and how these days it is measured. This was fifteen years ago and so I might have been way off. However; when I returned from Fort Lee, Virginia after the Colonel allowed me to remain in the Army, my so-called friends looked at me differently as if I had somehow become unrecognizable to them. They saw the ribbons and few medals upon my chest and claimed me to succeed. Even when I purchased my car they said,

"Man you most make the big bucks, because your ride is sweet!"

Today society seems to measure success by materiel possessions and that is the scale people are placed upon. That return home illustrated more clearly than when I had left we are a society that strives on "things" and the opinions of others. It is that valley of such lies we become trapped because too often we value the sanctuary of secularism even though we one day come to know that all our earthly securities carry no promises or surefire results. Time as this Author has mentioned is many things and specifically a Thief in the Night. In the wink of an eye all we have and know can be shattered like precious crystal falling from the table, or like cathedral stain glass window being shattered by a single stone.

That Full Bird Colonel reminded me that beauty and feelings of adequacy are fashioned with in the resilient soul. It is inside that dreamscape of Time's many illusions that the possibility of hope with in the fabric of the human condition fades away, almost the same as that perfect sunset over a quiet sandy beach. Finally, this Author also found that relationships can be and "are often" broken, while death is inevitable and will not wait because we ask it to. Real treasure is found beyond this life. I learned that from my mother who introduced me to the word of God. Only when real refuge rests on God and his ageless character can we face the obstacles this crazy life will make known to us. The faith, compassion and love for others that Full Bird Colonel demonstrated to a broken soldier from Somewhere Pennsylvania serves as a steadfast reminder to that truth.

Unrequited Love

"As I stood at the edge of my now flat world, the place where space and time seemed to fall apart, I faded into only a distant memory of who I felt I was destined to be. The heartbreak felt like someone close to me died or had been kidnapped by a thief in the late hours of nighttime. So yes, my world ceased to revolve the day the woman I loved and would lay down my life for decided she did not love me anymore."

I heard those words one evening what seems like ages ago and they have stayed with me nearly seventeen years later.

On September 11, 2001, at 8:45 a.m. the world itself seemed to stand still as a Nation's Wind was taken violently out of her lungs. America had not been dealt such a blow since the attack on Pearl Harbor sixty years prior. At the time; I had been employed at a Christian camp in Maryland and to be honest for me at age twenty and only a year out of high school it was an ordinary morning like all the ones before. Tuesdays were usually a reminder of the long week ahead. Mundane tasks ungrateful campers and yes believe it or not shady employers made me dread getting out of bed. It was also a reminder that at that point in his life this Author could not find his place in the world and was merely a drifter moving through the familiar landscape of just existing. The aftermath of September 11th, found this Writer one year later soldiering at a Nuclear Power Plant in response to those horrific attacks. It was while on that detail I met Sergeant First Class Camden Lawrence a fellow soldier from Erie Pennsylvania.

Camden and I hit it off quickly as we had a lot in common. Like me he grew up in foster care and his joining the military was more of an act of escape than an initial sense of duty. He was much older than me and had four children. Camden had been married for almost sixteen years and the way he talked about his wife you could tell how much he loved her, to the point he would lay down his life for her. He always talked of his children and how they "*were like arrows in the hands of a warrior*" because they gave him strength. It was during that nine or ten months stationed where we were that I would learn a life lesson like no other with complexity of relationships. This Author would discover that one of the most painful curve balls to be thrown in the world is a one-sided and unconditional love. For Camden it did not start that way. Once upon a time his wife loved him she said. The battlefield that Camden would find himself on was like no other storm he had faced and as I watched him fade away emotionally it broke my heart. He told me that after sixteen years of marriage he wife one day said,

"You are a good man and a great person. I love you as a person; I am just not in love with you."

I cannot even all these years later imagine how deeply her words pierced him. He had never abused her or stepped out on her and yet this storm was upon him. One night on duty as the moon seemed to dance in that October Sky and we sat in our Humvee; Camden broke down. He said,

"She told me that I was her ticket to freedom. If only she would have mentioned that back then maybe it would not hurt so badly."

Those opening words visited earlier followed as we talked to pass the time and stay awake. Mostly, all I could do was listened because I myself was not yet married. So, I just lent him an ear to unload his story. Still I now know that loving someone who does not love you might even be more painful than losing someone before it was their time. How does someone fight that battle? There on the battlefield of their heart the Fire Breathing Dragon of Unrequited Love becomes perhaps their greatest nemesis. Additionally, that battlefield I imagine is the most fragile. Camden changed that fall as his heart broke in ways I never saw even in my youth. Still, he held onto the hope that his unconditional love would prove stronger. He also said once,

I have always dared to believe that love should be the beginning and final act of one's very being. So, I choose to love even though it hurts, what a fool I must be" he chuckled trying to play the sadness in his voice off as though it were not there.

It has been nearly seventeen years since last, I saw him and so I do not know what became of him. What this Author does know from that memory is that being in love with someone who decides one day they just do not love you back is only the tip of the iceberg as it robs an individual of their self-worth, their value and sense of purpose. They sit around asking *"what is wrong with me"* when perhaps it was nothing they even broke, though it does not change the void inside of them.

Sometimes when I can sleep which is a task my mind plays back so many stories and paints so many pictures of another time. As those illuminations of my inner world become brighter because it is the realm where memories and dreams collide, I find myself slightly hopeful for some unknown reason. Perhaps, it is because like Camden I can still sometimes dream beneath the veil of the Future's uncertainty even if it is about impossible things.

As Time has marched on and life has placed me in the ring of adversity I have went twelve rounds with my back against the ropes when it has come to loving those who might never love me or moving forward from a broken past. It is in that ring I believe that voicing our emotions, rather than obscuring them beneath the stained quilt of denial only for them to explode at an unpredictable time, can help one accept that they are going through a painful experience but there is always a brighter day ahead. This is so especially when we find it hard to "go the distance."

As this Pioneer, this drifter traveling across the wilderness of life discovered, empathy is quite the companion and influences the hearts of men. When I think of Camden and even moments in my very own life, the reminders of the times it may feel like our pain is the only thing real in the world, is a lie. In that wilderness we ask about the storms of others we understand that we are not alone though it might feel that way.

Sometimes I wonder about Camden's wife's feelings and what brought her to that place that removed her love for him. She was not a bad person, nor was she evil or vindictive; she was just at war with herself. I dare believe that deep down she may have even felt awful everything. As I have moved through that landscape of time mentioned earlier I perhaps hope against the shadow of hopelessness that, when someone will not love you back it isn't because they are individuals who hates or wants to intentionally hurt the person who has loved them unconditionally rather than unrequitedly. The reality of Unrequited Love is real and this Author has seen it often. Someone reading this right now hears the candid echoes of such truth. To you whomever you may be, the spirit of resiliency comes when you remember that while you cannot always control your own feelings you can by stepping out of the ashes control your responses to those feelings which wage war on the battle ground of your soul.

Rewriting History One Day at A Time

The number One is a powerful number. It is greater than any other. Do you know why? I found it takes years to build trust much like a bridge. However; One lie can destroy in the moment the words left the mouth what took years to build. During the Civil Rights Movement while there were many fighting for equality One woman stood out by the name of Rosa Parks because she refused to give up her sit and started a bus boycott and furthered the movement. Only One Religion's Savior ever died for his people and it changed the world. Only One person can decide for you and me to move forward from the past and that is ourselves. I imagine what I am finding myself trying to say is that it takes just One person willing to step out of the ashes of the past so they can end a cycle of sorrow, pain, regret addiction or whatever chains bound their souls.

In 2004 my first son was born. Who would have saw that coming? I sure did not. I was only twenty-three years old. I recall calling my father saying,

"*I do not know how this happened.*"

His reply still makes me smile to this day,

"*I thought we had that discussion about how babies were made*" he said as he laughed.

The fear of failure pierced my confidence like the edge of a cold sharp dagger. I did not know how I was to be a father, at least not a good one. For much of my life the haunting whispers of "*You're Not Good Enough, You Never Will Be*" echoed through the corridors of my mind. Though I feel I did a fairly good job of obscuring those feeling from wife as I am certain she had many fears of her own; inside of me I was scared to move. I mean I worried about my son's future because I had learned that It can be a very frightening world. No, I knew it was a place filled with darkness. The fears of my childhood trauma becoming my son's reality not because of my wife or I, but because of people without morals or care taunted me. I mean what would I do if someone harmed my son the way I had been. I imagine I fear I would cross the line and revenge would undo the strength I had found through Faith.

While in the Hospital as my wife slept I held my son and found myself fixed upon his tiny face. I held gently with my hand his and the fear I felt slowly faded. I prayed as I held him and sang Jesus Loves me and prayed that God would reveal to me what a good parent was because I wanted to do better. I wanted to create for him a world without fear. Truth be told that is impossible. As I fixed my eyes upon his little eyes I knew I would die for him. Dreams of a happier, better world, became visible to me when I dreamed of all he might become.

It was not until the years began pass I came to understand there are millions in the world that did not have an architype of perfect parent to guide them. As I thought more about it, it hit me, there is no perfect parent. Now my mother was a soldier. I pushed her, I wore her down, but as I remembered the fact this woman took in two children and later took many more along with the man who would one day adopt me, I understood what a good parent was. They are there! They are in the lives of their kids during the failures and victories.

If I would break the cycle I had to believe that I could raise my son to be a man of integrity. The harder reality I had to learn was that my son is not me he is unique in every way. I knew I would have to let him fall and not keep my thumb upon his every move because that would be the only way to rewrite history as there is no learning without falling.

When I thought I had a handle on the daddy thing 2006 brought son number two and then in 2008 life stopped me on a dime and it appeared the world was falling apart for good this time. I will speak on that here soon. 2009 brought son number three and then in 2014 my youngest child came into the world.

All the fears of failure, the uncertainties of if I would break the cycle of a broken past remained to be seen. I look back at the years God has blessed me with to see missed opportunities and moments I can never have returned. One of the greatest discoveries I have ever made is that every one of us including myself, regardless of yesterday have something special and significant to put into the same world I said was filled with darkness so that perhaps light might shine through us.

For one to rewrite history, they cannot go back and change what was. We have talked about that a lot throughout these pages. Rather that powerful number of One, just one individual who dares to believe those scars they thought were the worst chapters in their lives becomes the very ink they use to write stories of hope inspiring future generations. For me I like to believe that my goodness in the sense of how I treat others will forever remain guarded by the shield of humbleness so it is passed onto my sons.

Rewriting history one day at a time is recognizing the mistakes of yesterday and allowing the wisdom from those moments to guide your choices so future generations will be moved by your bravery as well as your fight for something better for them and everyone who's life intersects with your own.

A friend once asked me what I thought my greatest life accomplishment would be. I thought for a moment and said,

"no matter if I every write a New York Best Seller, or perform the National Anthem again in front of thousands of people, regardless of where my career advancement takes me, it will all mean nothing if I fail at raising my kids and teaching them God loves them. Even if everyone I love turns on me and the world falls apart, I still want to be the one that put an end to a legacy of abuse and toxicity and give my children a future I once dreamed of."

I am not a perfect dad, but the one thing I am now certain of is that my love for them is. God's willingness to trust me when I did not trust myself gave me hope, that *"while our fathers sinned and are no more,"* and *"we bear their iniquities"* (Lamentations 5:7) through Grace we can rewrite history because of what we do today. I can find hope in the darkness because I learned to always be grateful for all the miracles God has allowed me to experience.

Miracles Are All Around Us

Many people I have encountered have asked me if I believed in miracles and all that they can bring.

"*Yes*", I say with certainty "*because I am living proof a fragile human being.*"

Sometimes when I am speaking or teaching Sunday School I have been asked if I believed in hope as it is a rare and simple thing. Again, I would answer,

"*yes, because it lives in me a fragile human being.*"

This entire journey has been a miracle because had I been asked those questions years ago I would have likely said no. Beyond the limits of what the eye can see or mind perceive this I know to be true as C.S Lewis once said, "*Miracles are a retelling in small letters of the very same story which is written across the whole world in letters too large for some of us to see.*"

The telling of my story and introductions to others this Author has met is an illustration that Miracles are all around us and sometimes when we go looking rather than have the Faith they just are, we find them but not in the form we intended.

I had not been married but maybe five years when my doubt not in God himself but His Devine Power would change my life forever. Before I visit that moment, I want to first say that from the day my biological mother robbed me of my childhood and later abandon me to die a miracle was already in progress. It would be sixteen years later that I would marry my wife, the love of my life and I would be given the chance to plant new roots, untainted by abuse or abandonment. Even in the storms I pray she knows I love her more than my own life. This point is essential because the memory I am about to share is not so much about my resiliency but that of my wife's even if she will never believe it.

I had worked several jobs since we were married and was often struggling with finding my place in the world so to speak. My timelines are off a bit but in 2008 my life would change forever. To this point my wife had been a soldier, from my loss of numerous jobs, to bad decision making and my suppressed depression. The storm she was about to enter defined her very character and love for me.

It was a Friday like most others. I had been working for about a year at a box manufacturing plant with my brother and was not doing that bad. I was ready for the weekend like most folks usually are. Yet, this would not be like any other Friday. As I was driving along route 30, I watched as the rain danced religiously off my windshield to a cadence I will never forget! There up ahead in the distance traveling at a fast rate of speed I saw two headlights which in an instance became one right in front of me. It was a motorcyclist now on a head on collision with me.

As I jerked the wheel I spun out of control. My car did a 180 through a fence and then came to bone crushing stop as I was wrapped around a tree. As my breathing became heavy I was sure that my life was in its final moments. I prayed for forgiveness for all I had done wrong. God and heaven knew those sins were ten thousand miles long. I could see what I believed to be a wasted life through the looking glass of regrets and chances not taken. Still, I prayed for my family because I knew there was a God. In the silence of that car I did not fear death for I knew it comes to us all as it is as inevitable as change itself.

As I became faint I remembered many of you from my past, but most of all I remembered this passage, *"But those who wait upon the lord shall renew their strength; they shall mount up on wings as eagles, they shall run and not feel weary, they shall walk and not feel faint"* ISAIAH 40:31.

About this same time, I thought I heard a whisper which I cannot explain

"Trust me, do not be afraid" the whispers uttered.

I know now that was God's voice speaking gently beneath the rain of that stormy night. The rescue crew arrived and after forty-five minutes cut me out of the demolished Buick. I was life lined to the nearest Hospital only to be told they could not help me. They still charged me eleven-thousand dollars for a few x-rays which they screwed up the first time. Anyway, I found myself in another ambulance now headed for Hershey's trauma unit where titanium was placed into my right leg due to the serious fracture of my femur. My leg was shattered into fragments of bone. Perhaps the pain medicine placed such thoughts into my head as I was thinking man…… there goes the dream of being an NFL superstar! I mean after all Big Ben and the Steelers needs me, right? They just did not know it yet. A running back low to the ground and built for speed.

As I said earlier I was blessed with a wonderful wife who soldiered through this with me. For months after I would be laid up in rehab, struggling with my inner demons and worries never realizing what my wife must have been going through.

Many nights I lied awake not realizing that in a way I asked for this. I recall asking God to speak to me like he did Moses and Elijah, that audible voice I longed to hear because I was human and weak and I allowed doubt to infect me. He spoke in that car as sure as I breathe. I asked for a miracle and my lame and broken body would be healed. My wife had signed papers for amputation as doctors were not hopeful I would ever walk again. One year after this life changing event I walked out onto Camden Yards Stadium raised my horn to the American Flag and preformed the National Anthem for the Oakland Athletics and Baltimore Oriels in front of thirty-five thousand people. During that ninety seconds of fame all I could think about was that in 2009 God still made lame men walk. The cheering of the crowd upon finishing was as faded as my doubts once were. I believed in God you see, just not the power He wielded.

I spent a month maybe more in hospitalization and a few more in rehab. The real point to this story however is this; we are here for but a time. It is a blink really and nothing more. What we do with it is so important because it not only affects those around us; but our very soul's destination. Worry, fear, regret, and doubt are bullies and agents of God's nemesis Satan. If you do not believe he exists then you also have fallen for the greatest lie every told in the history of the human race's existence. Just as Satan whispered in to the ears of Adam and Eve that same lie only told in a different way.

Had I died that dark rainy night I am sure I would have gone to heaven, but did I do all I could while I was here? Did I love all those who might never love me? Believe me that is a hard one! Did I forgive those I had been keeping forgiveness from? It is not enough to just be a Christian. We have been called to "be disciples." I joke around a lot but this is no joke. We must spend each day as though it would end because one day it will and our bodies will return to the earth! We must not be afraid to witness and love our enemies. As I sat in that car that not so ordinary Friday, I did not fear for my life, for I have always known it was not mine. Instead I saw the face of my wife in her beautiful white gown. I heard her say I do! I saw my son reaching up for me to pick him up and swing him around, I saw my youngest smiling in his mischievous smile and I knew I had been blessed and had a great life! Mark Twain said it best, *"There are only two ways to live your life. One is as though nothing is a miracle. The other is as though everything is a miracle."*

Pray It Forward

There have been so many individuals to whom this Author owes his very existence. Many have appeared in these pages regardless of if those interactions were good or bad. Through their lives and then closely evaluating my own I believe that each person has hidden inside the vault rooms of their lives, symbols from which we borrow hope when it seems unattainable or far from our grasp. I hope that those who wade through the pages of this narrative can borrow lessons from the stories with in it. It is one of my deepest prayers. Instead of just *"paying it forward"* I intend to pray it forward that those who are Guardians of the Ashes might step out of the place where they are.

Fatherhood changed much about the way I see the world. This probably more so than all those moments seen through that cracked telescope of time. Suddenly, much of what once mattered does not seem so important anymore compared to raising my sons. Though I have likely dropped the ball often, somehow, the world from the one I knew seems to have expanded and the storms facing our children have evolved differently than my generation did. Through watching my own kids grow and the brokenness of the juvenile delinquents I once worked with; as seasons come and seasons go, it is without warning adulthood knocks on the door to the future. How than do we step out of the ashes so our children might live to see better days?

My oldest has been making choices, taking chances, and facing disappointments as this school year was the first time he played football, and is his first year as a high schooler. I can remember that uncharted territory of my own adolescents and the fears it brought. The hope that collides with the hardships and discovery of personal innovation lingers in the hallways to coming of age. That inevitable fear that comes with the unknown, yet, there are countless opportunities to grow. So how do we prepare our children so they will not become Guardians of the Ashes?

When I am reminded of my life the answer stares me in the face again and again. It is through praying my children forward to God that their lives reveal with in me a newfound optimism about tomorrow. The very moments which have shaped and are still shaping my character came from the prayers of others. Somewhere along that rugged road of an uncertain life a kindness and truth was placed deeply along with a desire of who I longed to be one day. Why is this so important to the growth and expansion of the human condition? It is simple really, by helping others and becoming a blessing to them we are essentially helping ourselves. The very staircase which leads to becoming a Keeper of the Flames and moving beyond yesterday's unwanted sorrow begins with the way one thinks.

In a world filled with darkness and the many reminders of humanities sinful nature, there is hope. When a person steps out of the ashes even in their darkest hour; not that human nature has changed; it is because their view on the world and the way they see it have changed. Often, throughout the writing of this narrative the subtle whispers and reminders of a child left in a trailer with his brother, the individuals of immense character, even those who never won the day, serves as validation that it is through what we believe and think that chains are broken or fortified.

As I pray forward you all who are reading this narrative in this present moment, I ask God no matter where you are or what you think you always even in the darkest of nights; measure your worth in moments which made you stronger. In those moments that tried your soul whether it was an abusive past, an addiction, a loss or a current struggle which only you know about; that you would evaluate your scars because they remind you what you have overcome. Even the smallest of them often have the greatest value.

Wisdom has brought me to a place where when I look back, it is not the suffering that has the greatest impact on me anymore. Instead it is now knowing that even when I could not love myself or when those who were supposed to love me did not, God placed the right individuals in my life to fill in that gap. Like many I was caught up on those who did not love me I could not see those who did. Maybe for you reading this right now you say,

"no one loved me, they broke me, betrayed me."

Perhaps that is very true and all those things happened. This author is sincerely sorry if that was you, but I tell you the truth you are loved and you have value! I challenge you in this moment to look back once more and scan the vast landscape of your past to see if there was ever anyone who offered a kind word or even a sincere friendly smile. If in that place and time you cannot see a face I pray you know that you are the very reason I was inspired to write this narrative. You are loved even if we have never met.

Even if you are at that intersection where hope and hopelessness converge take heart. If you are not the praying type or even believe there is a God, I implore you again take heart. Even when the light at the end of the road doesn't always shine through when you need it, press on. The very lives you have read about and will still meet on the road head discover that Courage and Resiliency sometimes disappears when standing on the cliffside of what appears to be undefeatable personal difficulties. As they look down at their world below they might as I once did remain frozen in time as they try to grip on to the reality of so many heartbreaks and injustices. Sometimes they were the one at the center themselves.

As we prepare to journey into the defining of a Keeper of the Flame, it is essential to know that even though they have stepped out of the ashes, they too face every day struggles and challenges. Just as human nature does not change; neither do the unpredictable storms of life. Should you know one or meet one you will find that a universal trait sets them apart. A Keeper of the Flame takes those experiences which defined and molded them as their love and kindness to all they meet make them a blessing to many. Bear in mind this does not mean everyone will love them back. Their very character even in trying times is seen through the lenses of grace and goodness because it is their new way of thinking and seeing the world in which they live. Their relationships with others are built upon a strong foundation and they open doors of revealing to others that impossible is just a word that only carries weight if one believes it is so. The Keeper of the Flame are the open-hearted presences of one whose hope has been restored and pays it and pray it forward to the next person in need.

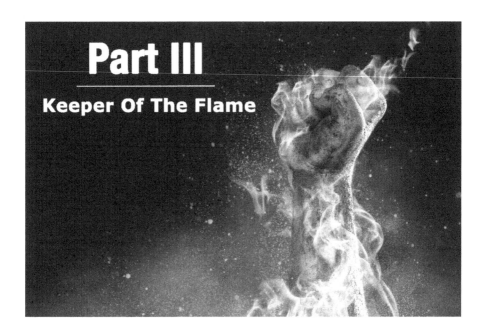

Part III

Keeper Of The Flame

"Learn to light a candle in the darkest moments of someone's life. Be the light that helps others see; it is what gives life its deepest significance."

— Roy T. Bennett,

Drowning in the Monocacy

When I was first dating my wife, I was becoming friends with her next-door neighbors. Michael whom everyone just called "Mikey" was like a little brother to my wife and her brothers. He was the adopted brother from next door I imagine you could say and he was growing on me too. He had this way about him. Before writing about Mikey I spoke with his mother who has become an inspiration to me and so many others. Mikey's mother is a living testament to the power of resiliency and the love of Christ as is his father. Michael's mother has been willing to allow share his story with you. She has attended adult bible studies I have led and I have seen through her the Spirit of Resiliency and it has fortified my faith. To begin, I will start with the son, Michael. I have found that sometimes God uses the smallest people to change the world, even if it is only the world of a few or one that only God sees.

As the years have passed the ripples of a kind-hearted, lovable, humorous child fifteen years of age still move through the hearts of those who love him, who call him friend still, and even to places where others never knew him but have come to through the legacy he left. Michael was as many recall never unpleasant about anything or to anyone which in these days is rare. Why is that? These days kids can be ever so cruel. I think I know though even if many may not agree with it, he lived his life like Christ and loved like Christ and so it did not matter who you were, you loved him. While, I did not know him as long as my brother in laws or my wife, I recall the basketball games, the airsoft wars in my mother in-laws back yard and the talent of a young soccer player. Most of all I saw the light I longed for many years ago in his eyes and through his smile every time I saw him.

Every day young people die. Sometimes it is from a sickness or a "freak accident", a life is lost and one more person will always be missed. It is one of Life's harshest schemes. I do not recall the day I only remember the call. I was working as a security officer at that County Court house I mentioned briefly earlier when my wife called and said that Mikey and his friend were missing. There had been a lot of flooding that year and I left work to go help search. However, when I returned home to change clothes I was told that Mikey had been found in the Monocacy River and his friend soon after. If ever life were to throw a blow; Michael's family took one that puts most people down for the count and perhaps almost did. I remember at the boy's funeral seeing the brokenness, the pain and I was reminded that the life I had claimed was such a struggle was nothing compared to the days that now lied ahead for Mikey's mom, dad and siblings or that of his friend's family who had also lost a son. I think it was the first time I saw my one brother in law cry as he tightly clenched his fist while sitting in the pew beside me.

It reminded of Laura's funeral too. For some reading this they might be asking a few questions. Let's start with the elephant in the room, *"why are you telling me this and what does it have to do with you?"* First, I would state that initially at the beginning of this narrative I clarified that I learned that life was not all about me, and second I tell this story to remember a young boy who mapped out a new trajectory for his mother and father who would reach beyond even them and into the uncharted territories of seeking souls.

That just one life can influence so many others so it eventually influences the hearts of men is a miracle even if no one sees it that way. Our mind holds our thoughts and our beliefs. The things we take into our minds each day, past, present, and future, all contribute to our thoughts and beliefs. What we hear today might stay with us for many years to come and that happened to those who knew Michael including his own parents.

Since his passing his parents began a scholarship program in his honor so others could share in the love of sports that might not have been able to otherwise. The fundraisers also served to share Mikey's love for Jesus with all who attend them. I spoke at one years ago, a paint ball tournament I think. Michael's mother whom I love dearly and is now a close friend said she never knew that Michael had such a spiritual love for the Lord until after his death. People would tell her different stories about him such as what his favorite song was and how he would ask questions to his peers about the Lord. Though when his parents did not realize it they did notice he had a different personality when he was involved with the church versus involved in family events. In both he was very happy, but also recognizably very different.

After his passing the change in his family was momentous as through the storm perhaps when they wanted to throw in the towel, they found God throwing it back telling them,

"Wipe your face and dry your tears because you are almost there" God's presence seemed to say.

Through the storm and over passing of the seasons the family found Mikey's best friend Jesus Christ or perhaps he found them. Michael's mother told me once that she used to think she was untouchable. Does that sound familiar? I used to think that too! Somewhere in the jungles of days gone by before the Drowning in the Monocacy she would drink to have fun and never cared who she stepped on to succeed. The Compassion I see these days were not in her vocabulary but she had many people who needed her support, advice and trust. The answer to another question my mother asked me Mikey's mother answers well.

My mother asked me one Labor Day Weekend when I was visiting my sister why I had trouble letting go of the past. Like Michael's mother said once,

"I was looking for what the world could offer me."

The reason I could not move forward was because I was looking down or back instead of forward and up to the one who fashioned us all and makes all things new, Jesus Christ.

Through reminiscing about Mikey's death, and just recently experiencing in the past few years the death of several of my other peers I understand that we should live each day to the fullest because tomorrow is not promised. The moments we make in that life well lived is remembered not because of what we said but because of what we did. Each day God grants us we need to value the moments we are living in right now just as Mikey did because he knew this world was not all there was and he did not take things or people for granted. Before the sunsets on the day we should make a steadfast effort to repair our relationships when fragmented and cracked because after today there might not be one more hug, one more kiss, one more goodnight, one more basketball game or airsoft battle.

Mikey's mother realized that she was in love with a "dog eat dog world." She said,

"When Michael died, and that is so hard to say, my heart changed. I felt different. It was like I felt the emotions of the people in my path now."

Life we discover happens, not just for me or Mikey's family and friends, but for all of us. Even when we may face some of the direst situations ever, others around us are too. It is unpredictable it is not prejudice and does not discriminate but what have discovered not just from Michael and his parent's but so many others; is that moving forward does not mean we forget, it means we live during that chaos and adversity.

Living is the most courageous thing one can do and in doing so you choose instead of living as lion thrown in a cage, to live free as a lamb in the meadow of God's grace and trust the Shepard to see you through every storm and break the chains that bound you.

Wax Images

It was later in my life, the more mature years of my existence I witnessed from a different perspective the harsh truth of nurturing a child. Through the no longer damaged looking glass of my earlier days I understand oh to well that it is never tranquil or simple. When a teen is violent, dejected, abusing alcohol or drugs, struggling with mental health and or engaging in other uncontrolled and reckless behaviors, it can seem overwhelming. I myself have felt exhausted from lying awake at night worrying about what will become of those youth I had been trying to help. Except for the drugs and other issues mentioned above, my own life paralleled those young people's personal storms. They were the Guardians' of the Ashes I had once been. The even more subtle struggle I came to recognize was that they were not even my own children and that in its self was a whole other battle I faced day in and day out which I imagine would one day cause me to leave the profession.

I remember asking myself, will those troubled youth I saw everyday find their way or will they fade into a forgotten memory like an old photograph buried in a stack of picture albums? Will they remember anything I said or did? I used to wonder when they returned home, who he or she is with, and what they're doing. Would they live beyond tomorrow?

When I was a Youth Development Supervisor, Clinical Counselor and Career and Technical Training Specialist; I observed parents who felt despair over failed attempts to communicate, the endless fights, and the open defiance. Furthermore; the inevitable collision of having to embrace the other side of that coin gripped me tightly. You know, the one where parents do not care about their kids. Instead they leave them to linger in the shadows of uncertainty and well-developed malice formed by the cold waiflike hands of neglect and relinquishment. My eyes once saw those who lived in fear of their teen's intense mood swings and explosive anger morphed into extreme cruelty. I once recognized each day I worked with those teens, from family conferences and my very own past that parenting a troubled teen can often seem like an unbearable commission.

The reality I came to quickly from my days working with at risk youth was that as teenagers avow their individuality and attempt to find their own identity, many experience behavioral changes that can seem uncanny and unpredictable to parents. I was once no exception to this in years long past. That parent's, sentimental, obedient child who once couldn't endure to be alienated from them now will not be seen within twenty yards of them, and welcomes everything they say with a reel of the eyes or the crash of a bedroom door couched with the sting of profanity. As a counselor and mentor of troubled teens, I faced even greater challenges. You see I learned from the years I spent doing the job and my own teenage years, that a troubled teen undergoes developmental, emotional, and cognitive problems beyond the landscape of an ordinary teenager's concerns. They seem to repetitively exercise at-risk activities such as violence, truancy, drinking, drug use, sex, self-harming, shoplifting, or other criminal acts.

While I myself did not tread in such waters I did understand the anger those kids felt. In addition; those youth, those Guardians of the Ashes exhibit symptoms of intellectual health complications like depression, anxiety, even eating disorders. I observed it every time I looked in the eyes of an angry teen who said with tears in his eyes,

"You will never understand, you don't know where I come from Lynch, you have never had to look over your shoulder yo?"

It was in those very moments that the memories of times long past, echoed whispers of a forgotten but not discarded yesteryear. While those remembrances seemed to birth themselves with in the once ignored recollection of my life's history pages now filled with black and white yesterdays, I am now a Keeper of the Flame and not a Guardian of the Ashe's. The lives of so many angry and broken youth seemed to mirror the very life I once lived as if they were almost replicas or even wax images of myself.

Long Drive Up Deep Run Mountain

Sitting here typing these memories onto this screen, an illustration of a Monday morning painted so clearly on the canvas of my mind's eye appears. That Monday morning from a now distant time unveils itself as I made my way up Deep Run Mountain to the Ascendency Advancement Secure Treatment Facility run by the Commonwealth. More commonly it was known as AASF for troubled teenagers. Through the trees the Sun seemed to peek in and out of the branches as if to say,

"*Now you see me now you don't.*"

It was almost as though the Sun was like a child playing peek a boo with his or her mother or father.

The drive was a relaxing one as the road turned and veered sharply at times through God's Country USA somewhere in Nowhere Pennsylvania. The fresh morning air brought back the memories of a time when life was not so full of chaos and strain from the stresses of responsibility. A time perhaps of innocents, but then as I have said often before it is those years long past in which innocents diminishes into the pages of person's individual history. Inevitably just as each day comes and goes people must come to answer for all their choices; every one of them. I was reminded of the days when I had stepped out of the ashes and rewrote my legacy under the marble ceiling of God's Grace and Mercy.

Finally; I reached the top of the mountain and though black and white like a rerun of "I Love Lucy" I can see myself looking left then right and left again as I proceeded up the road past the army barracks to make one final right hand turn. Like all the days prior I would lock my car upon parking and then walked a short distance to the building which had once been a hospital many years before and was now a treatment facility for at risk youth. The old but well-maintained structure is surrounded by barbed wire and its entrance controlled by security officers.

As my feet carry me through the front doors I wait until 6:38 am, swipe my badge, place my right index finger on the scanner and punch in for the day. The day has begun as and my morning begins by walking up the stairs to the second floor of the building. As I step on to the floor the faint echoes of a once uncertain future when I had been a Guardian of the Ashes reminded me why I pulled myself out of bed every morning. Those dim cadences of yesteryear steadily marched in an already crowded mind as if to say,

"Isn't this ironic?"

Matthias Canterbury

Becoming a Keeper of the Flame I discovered is about looking at others through eyes of grace and mercy. It is like undergoing eye surgery so the Keeper will see the world through God's eyes rather than that fashioned by the human condition which is flawed deeply. It recognizes that the Keeper was also once a seeker. For me doing this job, I myself faced the reality that like these individual's I was once lost in The Sea of Broken Dreams. The painted images of that Ocean called doubt and Fear of Failure reminded me of where I came from and where I was now headed. The thing about resiliency is recognizing other people's struggles. This cannot be over stated. It has become the drive behind these words. As C.S Lewis once said I imagine *"true humility is not thinking less of yourself; it is thinking of yourself less."*

Throughout my life I had a front row seat too such individuals' who seen dark days like I had maybe even darker. From my mother, to Brett, Laura the youth I worked with, and the reality of life's challenges define us based upon how we embrace them. Still without Christ it is impossible to endure. As I tell you all this I can see Mathias, one of my troubled youth. It was about 9:30 am that Monday which I have been called to share that the youth on my assigned floor had been transported down stairs to begin their day in the Learning Center or more simply put school. This Monday had been a good one so far as it has started off with no major issues. The nice thing about those Monday's was that I had the office which I shared with two other counselors all to myself.

This lucid dream, this memory if you will that I am sharing, replays the images of me turning the small lamp on my desk on and the ceiling light off as I sit down in front of my computer. Since I am a lover of music I place my favorite Chris Botti jazz album in the little cd player loaned by my boss and friend Tyler to ease the stress while I work. Once the music plays I pull out a brown dead file of a former client while "Indian Summer "plays softly in the background. Flipping through it slowly one page at a time I wonder about the individual inside of it. The picture on the face folio looks all too familiar and not just because he was my client. To be more specific it appeared to be a clone of myself years before. Somewhere through that vast corridor of hidden time I saw the loneness, fruitlessness, and vagueness of a tomorrow that might never come; through the eyes of fifteen-year-old Matthias Canterbury.

Mathias had been sent to the program for truancy and marijuana use, not as major as some of the other youth placed in the facility yet; still worthy of his presence. I picked up the phone to call the probation officer once in charge of his case to obtain information for Matthias's file. *"Ring, Ring, Ring...."* three rings in all.

"Hello Delanie County Probation, Santiago Adams speaking" The voice on the other end of the line responded.

"Yes, this is Mr. Lynch from the Ascendency Advancement Secure Treatment Facility calling about my former client Matthias Canterbury. I need to get his court order from you to place in his file."

"No problem I'll fax it right over. However; I have very bad news. Matthias is now being investigated for possibly shooting someone. He and some buddies attempted to rob a convenience store and the clerk was shot. One of his friends was killed while being chased by the police…. Ran right into the highway that one did" Santiago replied.

"Thanks for the update and I am sorry to hear this," I said in a low sadden voice.

Tomorrow found its way for Matthias but it would become a today of an uncertain and now even harsher future where the "music would be hard to hear. I hung the phone up while glancing back at the photo in front of me and shook my head as I was drawn once again back in time. The parallel existence of this fifteen-year-old boy raised in the harsh environment of the city collided with my own past which I shared earlier in this narrative. Though I never used drugs or turned a gun on another my life was broken by choices. Some of these choices were external and uncontrollable but many were internal.

Though we were of different faiths, different origins, and different backgrounds both of us faced the reality of an uncertain future. Matthias like me; found himself at the intersection of hope and despair, failure and success. Sometimes I wonder what Matthias life would have been like had he had a mother like the one who chose me even with all my flaws. Would he have discovered the hope to *"hear the music of the future?"*

Matthias was an amazing artist and a poet. He was gifted but no one ever cultivated his abilities which might have helped him step out of the ashes. Perhaps he might have found hope through Jesus Christ.

Chatting with the God of War

It was about mid-day on a Friday morning in mid-November, that I can recall young Aries Jackson being heard cursing at the top of his lungs from the far end of the unit I worked in the days I spent with at risk youth.

"You don't know where I come from dawg, I look over my shoulder ole head just to make sure no one will sneak me, so I will sneak em first, that's how I roll yo, it's me doing me!!!" he exclaims adding explicit verbs.

Aries though given a strong name was broken inside by the inflictions of society and darkness I once knew. The Anger within him was like a lion on the battlefield of his soul. He had lost his mother to cancer at age ten and his father was no bargain. A man doing life for the murder of three other humans in a drug deal gone bad. Aries…. such a sad story, as inside of him his name appeared to fit him well because "the God of War" raged with in him. No matter who talked to him or tried to coach him it was best to await the storm until the squall had ended. I remember looking at Aries and saw myself and then saying in a low tone……

"Let me ask you one question, define responsibility?"

Aries now calm hesitantly says,

"Um it's when you are responsible for something?"

I remember trying to smile at Aries because of his simple reply. In all honesty it was much like the answers I gave years before when I lived in Allentown.

"Such a safe answer Aries to safe really. How can you dream of going home if you will not jump into the ocean and swim out to the ship that will carry you there? Instead you are waiting for it to come in and I have learned my friend; it never will until you change the way you think! There are many ways to define it as I have come to learn this. It is the ability to respond appropriately in all circumstances. You do not need to be responsible to know what is right; you need only be responsible to do what is right. Knowledge without application is like a sail boat with no motor and no sails, useless and stuck in the ocean because it has no way to propel itself onward. Why did this start anyway?" I asked, but perhaps not in those exact words but along that line. Aries looking me right in the eyes exclaimed,

"Because I was angry and I do not like being told what to do. You want respect dawg you gotta give it! Do you know Mr. Lynch what my father's only real advice was to me?"

As I looked in to his eyes, I replied,

"No. Yet, I would be interested to know, but first, do I look like a Saint Bernard or Poodle?" I inquired.

"No Sir" Aries exclaimed with a confused look on his face.

"Then please do not call me dawg, my name is Mr. Lynch and I have always called you by you proper name got it?" I said with a smirk getting for a moment Aries to crack a smile.

"I got you Sir I meant no disrespect to you, you ariyht you know? Well as I was sayin bout my pops I'll tell ya Mr. Lynch what he said! I'll tell ya but you an't gonna like it, no sir not one tiny bit because you didn't grow up in da hood. He said never let no one disrespect ya cause you have to do you and when it comes to women get as many as you can and get em young! He told me a man takes what he wants and does what he wants! He never said I love you or anything like that. Love is for sissies." He concluded with a look of sadness in his eyes.

As I listened and can still hear the echoes of the past as I share it with you now; the thought process behind the actions and rage made sense even if agreeing with the modality behind Aries crimes which brought him to us did not. It was that day when inner city life collided with my small-town world I realized that a child or even an adult who imagines they are going somewhere acts contrarily than the person who considers he is going nowhere.

Aries was that kid deep inside whom believed he was going nowhere! I do not recall our exact dialogue but looking at him I remember saying something like,

"Aries when you find the courage to take responsibility for your life choices you will break the chains of your circumstance. Courage is not the absence of fear but the ability to overcome fear and you whether you wish to admit it are afraid of failing. You are afraid of being labeled your father's son. I know firsthand that just because someone has a biological parent and while they should still respect them, they are not defined by them. A man is not defined by the color of his skin, his origins of birth or even by what name he calls God. Rather he is defined by his character and the choices he makes."

That Friday ended well on the mountain and it had appeared a lesson in true responsibility was evaluated. Still how does one evaluate anger or teach another to tame it? Not the simple human emotion that all men and women know; but the uncontrollable fire forged in the chasms of a broken and dark past. The malice chiseled down to form such resentment for the world and all those in it, it is difficult to identify from the shattered pieces of one's life. In addition; how then can that fire be slaked when it has burned for so long and seared hot enough to melt one's hopes and dreams? It could easily be said that I like many in that line of work, were no more than firefighters battling the flames of yesterday's arsons caused by brokenness's and sin.

What of Aries? Well like many of the troubled youth I have worked with over the years, he did return home a few months later but within four weeks was busted for selling heroine and oxycodone to an undercover police officer. He was then placed in the adult correctional system. While in the establishment we heard he tried to commit suicide, and was retained to a state hospital somewhere in upstate New York where he will most likely never walk the streets of his home town again because of the instability of his mind and fear of changing the life he had known.

There were many days when working with those young people I questioned if I was making any progress or even affecting their lives. The inquiries of change's probability echo often in my mind just like the echoes of my own past use too. Still writing these accounts has allowed me to look back and recognize that transformation is not something that can be forced or pushed onto the shoulders of the person who does not long for it. Not real change anyway. There is no stepping out of the darkness without realizing you are in it in the first place. That change is merely tyranny and adhered to out of fear.

Unwritten Pages

On that horizon where my youth now remains unreachable in the physical form, I did not realize that an individual's personal evolution was the metamorphous of the timeworn to the fresh new day, and the shattered life to that of the mended soul. The realization that as the nighttime of yesterday became a new day, this Author now understood the truth that all things can change even in the darkest of situations.

Change and the overdue desire for a life absent of uncontrolled anger and fear took time to find its way into the deepest chasms of my soul as I have again and again tried to highlight. Still it did. It was not the lectures of…. *"You need to do this or don't do that."* Rather it was more of a feeling and longing. It had been the desire to belong and to feel as though there was meaning and sound purpose in the landscape of living. This is much of the reason I worked with at risk youth so many years later for the term of almost thirteen years.

As I sat in my office on a hot summer's day working diligently on a monthly progress report for seventeen-year-old Diego Aretino I noticed how similar our lives were to one another and yet so different too. I could measure this through the goals set for Diego; one being to grasp the importance of self-regulation and self-image. Self-regulation is that innate ability to govern one's emotions and attitudes and thus positive choices are made because of such ability. A Sentry of yesterday for sure as I recall many sessions with Diego where his current state resulted from what others had done to him but always like I use to do left out his own role.

Diego struggled with depression and anger management but his anger was never projected outward. In the facility he was a model resident who never caused behavioral problems. One could say he tried to fly under the radar. Instead he often internalized it. The difference between Diego and I was this. My anger when I was young was projected on things and objects whereas Diego did so to himself. He was a cutter. The sensation of digging into his skin with sharp objects seemed to act as a numbing agent to losing his mother from illness and his father to a drive by shooting. Often Diego would say….

"Mr. Lynch it isn't no big thing. It's my body and it's not like I am trying to kill myself or anything."

What do you say to something like that? Diego from the age of thirteen had been through eight foster homes and in three youth development facilities not to leave out homeless two months.

In one foster home he was often beaten and made to go without food as punishment. The years had made him numb and therefore the only coping he understood was self-harm. One day as I sat with him he asked,

"Sir…. how; does one begin to imagine tomorrow? I mean it never really comes. You always tell us that in group. How can I hope for it when yesterday has shown me that I do not really have a fighting chance?"

I replied,

"You know tomorrow does not come this is true Diego. As for yesterday, I imagine it lied. Regardless, it is black and white and has been penned down in the pages of our individual histories. We cannot go back or dwell on what was. There is no point in it for it remains and we still linger on. However; there is always today. Now that is something to look at. Yes, today is a gift!!!! Isn't that why it is called the present?"

"I don't know what you mean sir. After all I am from the hood" Diego replied.

"It's simple really and yet complex at the same time," I recall saying. *"Today is the beginning of the rest of our lives and that is the simple part because today reminds us that we can start fresh. It is the commitment however to change that is a bit more complex. It is for this reason that our human nature tells us that with change come loss and uncertainty. We fear what we are uncertain of."*

I did not know where those words were coming from but the verbs from years long faded seemed to make sense as they had been a product of my own life.

"What do we lose?" Diego asked as he gave his full attention.

"Take someone who has given up drinking; he or she loses the feeling of numbness that comes with being wasted. Therefore, the eclipse that hid their problems and emotions much like the moon hides the sun is now revealed and they must face them. After all, like the sun, it was only hidden, right? It was still there behind the shadow of the moon was it not? They lose the ability to obscure those undesirables as they to remain. Another good example would be the man who decides to make an honest living through a trade or career. He loses so called friends and easy money, but gains independence, respect, and health."

starring at me with wondering and yet candid eyes he said,

"I don't really want to go back to the streets, I want to live but if I go back I won't make eighteen. It's the unwritten pages of the streets" his shaky voice had resolved.

My heart ached. To think my life was so bad could not compare to Diego. Sure, it sucked my past that is, but his situation I could not understand or imagine. Looking Diego in the eyes with the determined glow of hope I responded with a philosophy life had fashioned through the wisdom of living day by day when I stepped out of ashes.

"Each day we are faced with decisions…. what do we do with our lives? To whom should we place our faith in, if anyone at all? Here is a secret wait for it, wait for it ok here you go…. don't place your faith in people they will let you down often and manipulate you to achieve their ends. Perhaps place your faith in God. Yes, I said it and I don't care if they fire me because it, it is true!! Have faith in yourself even when your courage is fading!!! As a young person I can recall the road ahead seemed so withdrawn and distant," I stated while remembering those very moments like they were the day before.

"Yes, yes, Lynch that is what it feels like!!! It's like, like you know um… a…" Diego searching his vocabulary could not find the words.

"A highway stretching for miles with no rest stops in sight. Then when you think it cannot get any worse the gas light comes on." I uttered.

"Yeah man like that!!!" Diego nodded in agreeance as he made intent eye contact with me.

"Often times Diego we yearn for what is in front of us, what we can grab right now in this very moment. The immediate need for gratification poisons us. Our blindness to the potential future outside our immediate situation prolongs our lack of vision to the endless possibilities that await us. Being faced with time in a secure facility more times than not; perhaps serves as an anchor for our pride pausing long enough to use our own thoughts to decide if we even want to change. Maybe if one were to ask themselves... is that what I really want? A reputation as a sex offender, pot head or gang banging homeboy. Granted some of us come from what is called a broken home where abuse is not foreign to young people because they witness it firsthand. Abuse in all its forms can destroy and tear away our foundation. But along the way have we not asked ourselves... is this the life I want, am I really a throw-away person. An outcast, an outsider, a drifter in an unfamiliar land who has misplaced all form of human reason and decency, someone who acts out of anger, who has no control over himself, a person who will only keep losing control whether inside jail or in society, always under the supervision of some guard, probation officer, or police officer? That is what you must ask yourself right now Diego!!!"

What I remember most about this encounter and why it sticks out to me was how intently he listened as if he was hearing hope for the first time. I did not know where all of these thoughts were coming from they just rolled off my tongue. Perhaps that was just me hoping to help him place a different story on unwritten pages. The reality of working with at risk youth is that while they are there, most of the time what they want does not line up with what they will do when they go back home.

The connection between a city kid from the streets and a counselor from a historical town seemed to be there and so I felt led to continue.

"So, Diego, to whom do you owe our loyalty? Where do you as a person draw the line between what's going to benefit you to create a life with real significance verses that life spent completely without control inside a prison like this one; where almost every moment of the day your life is monitored by everyone other than yourself? This is a question only you can answer, because no matter what others may tell you or what I may want for you, it is you and you alone that will make a difference in your own life! Today Diego, here in this office you can choose to take your power back to wake up to maturity, and start taking the hard road ahead outside your affiliations and block, or you can surrender and continue to let others do the thinking for you. It's your own life, your own story. There will be pages in that story where it hurts to read but who writes it? That is each person's decision to make. You need to make yours and stop placing the responsibility of your actions on others."

I realize looking back I once heard similar words in my youth from those contacting me when I would turn away. Diego sat in what seemed to be a trance, deep in thought pondering the choices he would make from that day on. I do not know what became of him. I dare to hope, to believe that even though statistically change is a distant and almost out of reach thing for such individuals that anything was possible. My life and others who defied such odds by God's Grace proved as much, so I believe he found his way but I may never know.

A Mile in Her Shoes

Solely to continue identity protection as has been my unwavering practice when writing or telling a story that has transpired; I felt led to share a story about one of the young ladies I once worked with. We will call her Grace because by Grace her life was saved.

Grace struggled with the all-encompassing fear of life. It was a different fear then one experiences from watching a movie or going to a haunted corn maze or house. It was a fear so toxic it prevents us from living because it dabbles in the *"what ifs"* the *"am I good enough"* whispers that fill our minds. Does that perhaps sound familiar? That fear that makes getting our everyday tasks done and clouds our minds and sets us on a collision course with our own self-worth. Fear that causes one to sink deeper and deeper into a suffocating darkness. Some reel under the pressure and give in to depression, anger, or hopelessness. Others wage a daily war. However; everyone who sets internal limits to his/her goals essentially buries his/her best qualities, and jeopardizes his/her innate talents.

Grace was a writer like me, but for her it was a gift rather than a talent because it just seemed to flow from her mind and into the poetry book she had been penning. There is something else that should be mentioned, no one just wakes up afraid, broken, or hopeless. They are learned from the moments which shape our lives. While Grace's poetry was beautiful it was also the blueprints of her life living on her own from the age of thirteen to the age of fifteen before anyone knew any different. I thought to myself how can one survive especially when they live in a rundown and forgotten part of a city where looking over your shoulder is an everyday common practice. As I would glance back at my own life I asked, *"could I have walked that long mile in Grace's shoes?"*

During group one Friday night we were talking about negative thoughts and self-fulfilling prophecies when I was greatly challenged. It was around the subject I think of understanding that just as negative thoughts and words have the power to lead us down dark paths to undesirable destinations, positive views and words have the influence to guide us through oceans of inspiration and hope to a destination of joy and fulfillment. That's when Grace raised her hand and said,

"all that makes sense if we had positive things to think about when all around us the world is falling apart. When those who were supposed to love us throw us away or lying on the floor every Thursday night keeps you alive because of the violence. How Mr. Lynch can we find something to be empowering or inspiring, when we cannot let go of what is our reality? The reality of Fear and broken dreams and replace it with something better."

That Grace was right and I had no answer. Not one that would matter. I have heard often and I have probably said it myself that we are defined by what we do not by what has been done to us. While even now that all things can change for the good, for some it will be a harder fight than others because each individual wear their own pair of shoes. Until we walk a mile in theirs we will never understand the forces they are dealing with.

Let's look at Grace for a moment more. Her father would beat her and then one day he just never returned. As for her mother she had died from a drug overdose when she was ten or eleven and so, it was just Grace and her little sister. It was not until she sold drugs and the only other thing she had that brought her to our facility, her body. It is that moment which might have been what saved her.

During one of our creative writing classes I would hold she shared about broken dreams. I understood "the why" she did what she did even if it was hard to digest. Human tendency is to look down upon others rather than help them to their feet. We are a race of judgmental minds especially if the mold of another does not align with our own. Now, not always is "the why" a justification for the action but knowing it builds the foundation for empathy. I realized from her story and those of so many I knew including my own; it so great to have dreams and aspirations. They give you hope, something to look forward to and to plan for. Those dreamer's dreams can bring the fruition true living. However; when the dreamer no longer remembers how to or was never taught to dream of such things they are not living, only existing.

One of Grace's writings remain with me specifically as she outlined in a very rhythmic way one of the *"Breaker of Dreams"* and looking back that would have been an awesome title for a poem or story. She wrote about the power of the tongue and how it can both destroy and heal. I understood where she was coming from because still today almost at forty I bare scars inside from things once said. So, what if what we hear is something negative about us? What if we believe it too? Grace as she read to her peers told them that what we believe about what others say has the power to steer us in an undesirable direction if we let it. Wow! A fifteen-year old girl from a "City of Forgotten Dreams" recognized one of the key "Breaker" of hopes and dreams.

Grace left when she was eighteen years old. While with us she found two new desires. One she wanted to be a writer and second she wanted to join the military. Now since she came to us as a juvenile she could enlist. Many of my peers did not believe she would because the recidivism rate is always in flux and not in a positive light. However, I made that mistake once before with another youth whom I did not believe in and he did what he said he would. I remember his postcard which read "thank you for believing in me" when really, I had not. I will speak of him soon. So, I dared to believe. Some years later by accident or maybe not I ran into Grace to discover she had spent the last four years in the Army as a Journalist and came to know Jesus as her personal savior. She told me her life was forever changed and that after joining the military and leaving that broken city she finally lived. What is resiliency? I know I keep coming back to this but individuals like Grace remind me of what it is.

For those of us who have been in the fire, who have been touched by the flames, resiliency is not just waking up one day and just conquering all that lies behind us or before us. It is a process we must accept may be lifelong so we can become like a river always moving forward and never staying in one place and never going back. Unless we can remind ourselves of this inevitable truth we will forever remain "Guardians of the Ashes". I have discussed with my own boys what it means to live a life worth living. While they have not suffered loss, abuse or any significant hardship yet, I hope it prepares them for storms which are inevitably ahead.

Sometimes my oldest son Isaiah will tell me something is too hard like football, a class he is dealing with, or a story he was trying to write. As I look back through that telescope of years gone by, I wish I would have followed my own advice.

"Isaiah" I said once; *"Imagine if every day we woke up inspired to fight for what we want most with the attitude that there is nothing that will keep us from that desire except ourselves?"*

I do not know if he understood but he smiled at me and that was enough.

The Road

Throughout my life I have often heard that life is but a road. I have found this an appropriate metaphor as I think of all the people I have met and lost along the way but also all the people my life has yet to intersect with by God's Grace.

There is a universal truth about roads. For starters they often connect one place to another. Some are longer than others while some seem to end too soon. There are many crossroads and intersections where highways collide. Whether the road be long or short this can be said. This idea that Life is a highway of its own reveals many similarities to the actual ones we use for travel as we go about our day to day.

Many turns veer sharply and dangerously left and right. Countless times, the fog of doubt and uncertainty forms a cloud upon the horizon. There are many forks and wrong turns that take you miles away from where you had wanted to go. Let's not forget those mountains and valleys that seem to reach into the heavens and sink into the void! It appears the road is endless and without purpose because it seems to extend for miles through the vast desserts of obscured empathy or in the highlands of apathy. Like those signs that say, "rough road ahead" or "uneven pavement" such is the journey that is life.

However; it is because this road symbolizing one's life, this too can be said. We never need go it alone! For the one in whose image all men were made rides shotgun as we make our way along. He is there to grab the wheel when the turns become too hard to navigate! He becomes our eyes when the fog becomes too thick! He pushes us when the mountain's peaks seem to pierce the clouds.

When we sink into the valleys and those shadows of despair He fortifies us because He loves us! I have seen those I love, hold on to that very hope even when it could not be seen by their human eyes. They held on to the steadfast belief even in their darkest hour that God's plan has its purpose even if we cannot see it or understand the suffering it is written in.

This road I have been speaking of throughout this entire tome finds me looking back at the many mile markers where other traveler's engines left them sedentary. There are nights I sit up like this one trying to understand why at mile marker five Highway 86 I was left sitting in that trailer for five long weeks. This thought, resiliency….it is an inner strength that is the gas in our tank so to speak. Sometimes that car breaks down for reasons we cannot control, it perhaps is where we stopped. Still I wonder about those like Laura, Brett, Michael and friends I went to school with not so long ago what they would have become had the road allowed them to journey further.

As I reflect on these thoughts I now take every day one at a time. I now see life in a whole new way. My own journey through Faith has brought me to this steadfast conclusion. All of us no matter the length of our road or even how we may have traveled it, God forgives us if we ask! This road/highway we call LIFE during its chaos and pain is a blessing because we could travel it and even more of a blessing just knowing that through Jesus Christ God rides with us and desires us all to call on Him when the road becomes ridged in Jesus Name. I do believe that "joy comes in the morning" and I understand with all I have endured there is always someone facing a bigger Giant.

"Candles in the Wind"

My friend Reggie and I sat in my office talking about the long week. Our conversation led to our weekend plans and then the dreaded staff meeting we would have that Monday when we returned to work. One colleague named Sonya was always an individual who did not come across as the social type but seemed often to keep to herself. Regardless, she was a hard worker who always got the job done and went above and beyond what had been expected of her and she never lingered in the sea of complaining as so many of our colleagues and even I had done. Though not very athletic; Sonya worked a lot with the outdoors programs which elicited from youth the ability to channel their anger, fears, and frustrations into exploring nature and even overcoming fears through obstacle courses and wall climbs.

Rarely did Sonya smile but she never had an unkind word to say. When she did have a conversation, or facilitated a group session she was intelligent and though she never said it seemed as someone who went through the storm, I could see her past, though I did not know what it consist of. Only the images of one scarred in her lifetime revealed themselves because it was something I once knew well. Occasionally it was little things she had said, almost as though she were longing to tell her story, a story many of us who worked with her will never know.

That Friday as Reggie and I sat in the office Sonya had come in to join us. She sat down and had an unusual sunny disposition about her which was out of character. She was overly happy and I imagine we just thought maybe she won the lottery or found a boyfriend. Perhaps our employer finally gave her the raise she deserved and needed. However, this was not the case. Her happiness was a smoke screen to the truth. What I can recall from one of her groups with the young ladies she mentored was how she told a story of a young girl she once knew along with the girl's difficult home life.

It was a tale that pitted Maiden against inebriation and exploitation and how those patterns were quickly steering her toward an empty future. The Maidan of the tale spent nine months as a runaway sleeping on the streets and in an out of missions and shelters. She was confronted with homelessness at an age where most are struggling with fear of failure in school sports and homework assignments. It was a story of another time and another individual. However, it was not until later I wondered if it was a chapter torn from the pages of Sonya's own past. As a writer, public speaker and creative thinker, my creativity comes from real experiences in my life. This narrative is the very example of that.

Once, I can recall her dealing with a youth who was a cutter and her telling that youth that in her own life she had dealt with hardship and failure. Her family was poor she had said and she had to cope with suicides, mental illness, and domestic violence. These things looking back paralleled the story of the Maiden she had known years before. She told of how two of her family members died of alcoholism and how someone close to her took their own life. I do not know how I could not see the story being written on the pages of another's life write before my eyes. No one could see the hidden messages either of a life whose candle was fading fast.

It was on Sunday night I received a call telling me not to come in to work Monday for the meeting that Reggie and I had been dreading. When I had asked why the heartbreaking news was delivered. Sonya was found dead in her apartment hanging from a beam which pointed to suicide. I've had other friends attempt and even family members complete suicide. That intersection where so many people have come to where hope and hopelessness collide, remind me of that time years ago where thoughts of running into the road danced so religiously in my mind, but how the kindness of another perhaps prevented this. Laura, I love you because you changed my mind.

I place this memory into the fabric of this yarn not to initiate shockwaves of sympathy but to stress that suicide is a real and tragic thing that goes beyond an individual being merely a Guardian of the Ashes. They become Shadows of themselves and eventually the ashes they once stood Guard over. Like candles in the wind their light fades and eventually blows out. So, the modality behind the why of my remembering Sonya and others left unmentioned is also to stand in the gap and speak out for mental health awareness. For anyone reading this who has had to cope with this or has even contemplated suicide; I share this as another way to encourage others to feel not so alone in their struggles. The bravest thing and often hardest thing anyone can do, is to live!

I see the faces of those I have lost and that I have known and today in the present moment which these words find their way onto my screen, I want to honor those of you enduring through losing a loved one to suicide. While the sorrow, the feeling of responsibility, and the intense sadness never goes away we move forward as best we can and often only through the Spirit of Resiliency. When this manuscript was being fashioned my own family endured the loss of a loved one at the hands of suicide.

While I was working as a Supervisor on a mental health unit years ago I faced the realism of those struggling with suicidal thoughts. So often many of my peers would comment like, *"oh there just doing that for attention."* Or more notably they would talk amongst themselves when they thought no one could hear them and make remarks, like *"the world will not be worse off if so and so offed themselves."* Now to clarify it these were a few select individuals in the business of earning a paycheck and clocking out. They never lived in the world some of these kids did.

One Saturday night my worst fears came to light. The fear that a youth would attempt suicide while on shift and in charge of the building; made my stomach rumble. Now this individual and I for the most part had a decent relationship. Most of the time, he only made threats, but never demonstrated the will to act upon it.

Raised in a rundown part of Pittsburg, the eighteen-year-old who we will call Donavan suffered from bipolar disorder. At least that was the diagnosis. Like many of the youth I had worked with, drugs, violence and harming others was the anthem of his learned life from the streets. When he was angry he would often attempt to break the facility's equipment or antagonize another youth. Each day was cause, to remain extra alert while Donavan was at the facility. That haunting and unforgettable Saturday night would set me on the desire to find a different career path. That night changed me forever. It was the intersection where the weight would become too much to carry. While roaming the hallways from unit to unit a coworker's terrified voice was heard across the radio,

" Code Red, Code Red,"

The layman translation means, immediate support needed, life or death situation.

Upon arriving to Donavan's room, he had somehow tied his shirt around his neck and to the post of his bed tight enough that his face was turning blue. In the moment everything seemed to happen so fast. Thousands of scenarios were running through my head as we tried to untie him from the bed post. Even while suffocating from his make shift noose he fought us while he wheezed and let out the partial words,

"I want to die, let me be, let me be"

A choice had to made and I knew after this night, the next job I took I did not want to be the one to ever make such a call again. Call me a coward or a fool but I had to leave the field. I would never be a supervisor again! Knowing I would likely lose my job I instructed one of my coworkers to get the handcuffs. They argued with me because we had a protocol but I could live with the consequences if Donavan did. Even though this was against procedure I could see no other way to get him to stop struggling. After his hands were cuffed we could cut the shirt from the bed and remove it from his neck.

When I look at our lives, humanity; we are all like candles in the wind. That once upon a time when my life seemed so broken, the thought of living in a world like Donavan's reminded me there is always someone else out their who's battle is far worse. The wind blows where it wants to and sometimes it blows so hard that the flame dies out. If ever you look at everything that has gone wrong in your life, I challenge you to ask this question, *"what are the struggles of others right now? What is their story?"* You might find that perhaps even with all that had gone wrong or the scars you bare are nothing compared to another.

Merely Existing

There was a point in this Author's life where he had learned from his own past and through those he worked with daily that abuse and the scars they leave lasts for a lifetime. Even at an age when children become teens, child abuse affects every decision, every opinion, every reaction they make. Guess what? The same is true for adults! It was through the worn hour glass of Time I have found that my past became part of who I am much like a birthmark or a shadow that spans an entire life time. Once it takes place it never goes away. It is how one copes that makes or breaks them and I imagine that has been the main hub of these pages. Meet Calvin. Even though he was probably the toughest kid I ever worked with my heart ached for him most. Calvin had learned to live with savage beatings and solitary confinement. He once told me,

"I was locked in closets for days at a time while my mother partied, beaten until I looked like a rainbow, whipped with electrical cords, but oh how I wanted mother to love me. Stupid woman! I wish she loved me, but none of that matters anymore and yet I still love her"

For me those words were spoken so long ago and yet it has never left my inner awareness. Calvin had run away again and again until he had nowhere to run. He had been in a foster home where he was raped by two males and forced to sleep in the garage with only a dirty blanket. For a time, he lived on the streets of Somewhere, Pennsylvania from age fifteen to age seventeen. He was one of those youth that had taught me what it meant to be truly broken and defeated, past the intersection of hope and right into the valley of apathy and disregard for life. Like many ships beaten and battered he found himself on the Island of Broken Dreams.

This young man's way of coping with reality and the world was heartbreaking. Day in and day out while Calvin resided on the mountain he would eat and swallow pens and tiny objects hoping to die. His sense of empathy for those around him was nonexistent and in his mind, he merely "existed." How does one even understand hopelessness on such a scale? How is it that the checkered quilt of apathy woven by the tainted threads of a Sociopath's fingers; is folded so neatly in the locker room of one's mind with not even a hint of how it was placed there. Calvin was a different breed of teen one I hand never encountered before or have since.

I share this story because when one looks through the dark corridor of tragic circumstance and hopelessness even then perhaps their life does not seem so bad in comparison. On that horizon where a new-found reality sets in that reminds us there is and will always be another somewhere in the world who knows far better the weight that comes with such brokenness and hopelessness.

During Calvin's entire childhood he kept wishing something normally acknowledged as bad would happen to him so someone would understand why he was so hopeless all the time. He told me after a physical intervention that,

"looking back, it's probably strange Lynch, but I just thought that if something terrible happened at least I'd have a valid reason to be depressed and suicidal. My greatest dream was that death would take me away, not mainly because I thought that it would be better but easier because I would be gone!"

Death never came on its own but Calvin through actions and behavior offered him an empty room in his soul. For the life of me I could not understand even in a world with all its problems and sins that a fifteen-year-old at the time could be beaten by meth addicts fronting as foster parents and then fashioned to believe that he caused his own torcher. Calvin never had a chance where as I could have easily been him. It was days like these that seemed to try my soul as I could not imagine such evil could exist. Not Calvin but that which had been forced upon him.

I tried often as best as I could to reach Calvin and help calm his anger and suicidal tendencies through empathy and coaching but the bus of reason and reality had left that stop long ago. The images of my last physical interaction with him plays in my mind occasionally. During another intervention after an attempted hanging from his bed, Calvin screamed and cried saying,

"I wish I would die. Hit me! Hit me!" he cried out *"I wish you would hit me and leave bruises like the "normal" abusive families I knew."*

I looked over to my friend and coworker Tyler who just finished placing mechanical restraints on Calvin's wrists because in that statement Calvin identified our facility as his home and those who worked there his family. He was sent to s Psychiatric Hospital in Northern Pennsylvania and I never saw him again. However, a few months later I received a letter in crayon from him and the words touched and broke my heart simultaneously and it read.

"Hey Lynch, I am still alive. Imagine that. I just wanted to say thank you and I am sorry for all the times I hit and spit on you. You were one of the few good ones."

Not much else was written on the wrinkled paper with wet spots that could have been tears but I do not know for sure. I wonder how life might have been different for Calvin had he been rescued long ago. The one thing that is certain life does not discriminate with struggle. I wonder if you are reading this right now if you have endured if your outlook on adversity has another perspective. I know those years working with the kids changed mine as they had been places I never found myself and pray I never do.

"An Angel Closes Her Eyes"

When I was still in Highschool I met Layla. She was beautiful, compassionate a loving spirit. Little did we know a short time later she would begin an epic battle with cancer.

Layla's life, the way she rejoiced and praised God even though losing her battle with cancer reminded me that The Spirit of Resiliency is realizing that Courage is not the absence of fear, but rather what takes place when we face our fears, and endurance is not the absence of mountains or storms, but rather what takes place when Courage tells our soul this is not the end! She was little bit younger than me when she died leaving behind her husband and children. Yet, through the pain and suffering the light that seemed to radiate from her still illuminates the hearts of those who loved and knew her.

Many people are facing uncertain futures and diagnosis. Perhaps, it is you and you are reading this right now. Layla and others, I have had the honor of knowing reminded me time and time again that even during such a storm there we find the courage to still inspire those around us and the quality of our lives improve and we are better because of it. It is an easy thing to lose especially when our circumstance is likely certain but that separates the Resilient Spirt from the average person just trying to make sense of everything.

Layla never stopped telling her husband and kids she loved them nor were any of her social media posts written to bring others down but gave them hope. On that day when Layla left this earth an angel closed her eyes only to open them so the first thing she saw was Jesus Christ who had gave her the strength and courage to face the earthly journey she was on.

This life has shown me many things and one I believe is that while death is inevitable it is never the end regardless what the world says. In those losses which I have been a part of I have learned there will always be times when we wish our loved ones were back, but, we must believe and remember that they are only in the other room where sickness and death have no place.

Believe me when I say I know it is hard to look at life this way but the Spirt of Resiliency does not always mean we physically win the battle or battles we are fighting. It is something many cannot and may never see. Layla's life and her courage in the wake of the storm reminded me that happiness is found not in the length of life but rather in the quality of it and the love we give to others above ourselves. I love you my friend and will see you again.

The Rhythm of a Heartbeat

It was many years ago that I first met Marion. I was staying with her family for what foster homes call respites. My mom was working a lot to keep food on the table and so I stayed with Marion and her Grandparents often and it was like a second home. I never knew that the years would bring us as close as they have. She is like my sister, no she is my sister and I love her very much and pray she feels the same. Her story speaks to the very nature of what this book was meant for, The Spirit of Resiliency. However, it is even more. It separates a religious person from the righteous one. Religious individuals I have discovered praise God when the sun shines bright, but the righteous one praises Him when the storms bring strong wind and unforgiving hail. Marion, she is humble but in that humility a righteous woman.

At thirty-nine she would begin a second life. It is by God's grace she is with us and the significant chronicling of her struggles and how she endured them will echo through my soul all the days of my life. My sister in Christ and friend was born in 1979 with a condition known as TGA, or Transposition of the Great Vessels. In other wards she was born with a backwards heart. Many children born with TGA need immediate heart surgery to save their lives. Marion was very blessed to not need surgery, because her condition was congenitally corrected.

Each heart beat has its own rhythm a friend once told me. Its Cadence is unique from others. Marion's heart's Aorta and Pulmonary Artery were doing each other's jobs. The Pulmonary Artery is supposed to drive blood to and from the lungs. The Aorta pumps to and from the whole body. Her weaker artery was having to do much more work than it was designed to. Imagine for a moment being in a manufacturing plant on a line assembly where each station must complete its task before you can complete yours and to finish the task on time you now must run three out of five stations on your own because everyone called of sick or quit at last minutes notice. The work still needs to be done so there is no way around it or the company loses profits for not meeting their quota's.

Marion lived as normally as the rest of the kids at school, so this heart issue didn't affect her. To be honest I never even knew she had a condition until years later when I would be praying for her heart literally. She had only signs when she shoveled snow, or ran the mile every year in PE class. Though she pushed herself she almost always came in last because she couldn't breathe, and her heart would pound so hard.

The same year I graduated from high school in 2000 and was trying to figure out where my life would lead Marion had finally figured out what path should take in her life. As I found myself in another military establishment Marion met Ray. She had dated him for years, but this was like the "love at first sight" you hear about in the movies. Marion was going to Aesthetic school somewhere down south, and Ray had joined the Police Department. The storm coming not too far on the horizon defined not only the resiliency Marion would reveal but that which Ray would too. I have never met him but the strength and love he would provide for my dear friend and the courage it would take to face uncertainty defines what a man is. He provides for and loves those God has blessed him with even when troubled waters are on the horizon. I hope someday to meet him and express that to him.

A little over a year later, Marion was working in a salon and felt ill. The fingertips of nausea, the nemesis of gaining weight, constant coldness, and the hot breath of exhaustion wore her down and took its toll on her body. This transpired for a few months and caused her to leave her job and the medical center she went to wasn't helping.

That sense that something was not right echoed through her body and she finally asked her parents to make me an appointment with her Dr. The minute he saw her he told her, *"Be ready to spend some time in the hospital."* She was taken to Hospital and treated for Congestive Heart Failure. Over time, her heart became weaker and could not pump blood, the heart failed and she retained many pounds of fluid. While in the hospital she also suffered a stroke, which thankfully by God's grace she recovered from with no lasting effects.

That stroke would be the intersection where her illness transported her to Johns Hopkins, where she met her Dr. At that time, he was Chief of the Heart Transplant Unit. Marion told him she wasn't having one of those, so he could leave. Well, she was wrong, and he is still her Dr. sixteen years later! After two weeks Marion was released. She went into the hospital at 140lbs I believe, and left around 100lbs. That's a lot of fluid! It appeared the storm had passed but as I have learned there are always more of them and whether we are ready or not we enter them.

For the next fourteen years they were wonderful. Marion was on medication and a low sodium diet. She and Ray married, and had a great life going! On July 31, 2016 Marion and Ray's world was rocked when she went into cardiac arrest in her kitchen. As I said there is always another storm. It finds us sometimes often when we are unaware. We never see it coming until we are in it's wake.

God placed Ray in Marion's life not just to be the loving husband he was but to save the life of the woman he loved too. Ray performed CPR for seven minutes while waiting for medics. My friend was literally dead, but after the external defibrillator shocked her she woke up and it was as if God breathed life back into her lungs. For a minute I want to point something out. CPR is a tiring process let alone when it is someone close to you the fear of losing them can over take a person but Ray remained strong. I am sure after it was over the reality set in. That alone to remain composed and not give up when fatigue set in is the character of a Resilient Man which is rare these days.

Marion spent a week in the hospital in a little pain but feeling good. She had an ICD implanted to help if this happened again. Like mother nature the winds of life would blow harder and with more intensity but it is the optimism of two faithful people reflected in the lakes of yesterday that I am compelled to share my friend's story. In April 2017 the defibrillator fired due to a VTach. After this incident, she felt herself deteriorating and fading away physically. It was I believe around this time she was also being listed for a heart transplant. Marion was placed as a status 2 which meant she was gaining time on the list while being home.

The heart failure was making it problematic to work, and so again she had to leave her job. Marion visited a heart failure clinic in her hospital often to receive IV medication to help eliminate the fluid buildup. Eventually that treatment stopped working. The walls seemed to get higher and higher to where it pierced the clouds and yet my friend did not lose heart in the sense I am using it now.

There comes a time when people realize decisions must be made even when they are hard and the outcome is uncertain. It reminded me of the papers my wife once signed to have my leg removed after being run off the road and thrown into that tree. Marion knew it was time to be admitted so they could move forward with the transplant. She had a SWAN Cath inserted into her neck and I cannot imagine that pain. This Cath was used to measure heart and lung pressure, and blood was taken from it. It took a while to be used to it,

"but eventually" she said, *"it was just part of me!"*

Marion lived in the hospital for thirty-five days. I remember watching the count down on Facebook and the prayers I prayed and all those who loved her prayed, that God would provide her with the heart she so desperately needed. However, the thought crossed my mind this would mean someone else would have to die so my friend could live. I prayed still knowing that God sees beyond my line of sight.

On May 10, 2018 Marion's Dr. came in to tell her there was a heart for her! Surgeries like this are not taken lightly and anything can happen so before one goes into the OR; the surgeon must look at the donor organ to make sure perfect for the recipient. Marion was rolled into surgery that day at 4:30. As prayers from all walks of life and parts of the state and perhaps other states flew heavenward Marion went under the knife to receive a gift from someone she had never met.

She woke up in the ICU and a nurse removed the breathing tube.

The pain was unbearable, and she was so nauseous that she couldn't even take the broth from the liquid diet! That pain did reveal one thing though, she was alive! After moving to the step-down unit things got better. She ate food that wasn't the best! Walking was also a big deal. Before her transplant she would walk around the unit often each day to keep her legs strong.

In the ocean of this storm Marion could see others waiting. Waiting for a chance at life with the rhythm of a new heart beat. There was a man, we will call James who received his heart the day after she had! A month later, a woman we will call Carrie received hers. Resiliency and relating to others comes from being in the same situation even if the way we face those situations differ. It brings people close to one another and that is what becoming a Keeper of the Flame is all about. It is in some people's darkness being the light that offers them hope where maybe there was none. Marion and Ray too were that light. My friend joined such a large, loving, and supportive group of transplant survivors!

She still knows nothing about her donor yet. However, she plans to reach out and prays that they are open to meeting her. Marion allowed me to share her story because not only through her did I see that light in which Resiliency shines like the Northern Star but because the willingness of organ donors not only saves lives like Marion but reveals the compassion that still dwells with in the landscape of humanity and such compassion is a driving force in developing the human condition which reminds us that in a world of so much suffering one heart's rhythmic beat can change the world.

Marion told me she wants to meet the family of the donor because she now has their loved one's heart! The generosity of this family saved my friends life. I know Marion, Ray and all who prayed, even those who did not believe in God but prayed, are eternally grateful and love them even though we don't know them.

That donors heart was hers. That beautiful healthy heart which I know Marion will cherish and protect for as long as she is alive. My way of thanking God and that donor is to share this story with you. Resiliency comes in many forms and not without some loss, that is the very nature of change. Organ donation is more than giving a piece of one's self, it is becoming an Ambassador of donating life. In a world filled with suffering, sorrow and pain the ability to save life if given the chance rather than destroy it allows one no matter where they have been too see the possibilities of where they can go or how they can make a difference in the world. This world needs more generous donors! People are dying while waiting!

Marion's story is a reminder of the possibilities that lie with in humanity's courageous acts of selflessness. Simultaneously there are those facing that uncertainty not all able to withstand the storm. Some break beneath the wake of such waves. However; it is the Keepers of the Flame like Marion that regardless of what outcome may await do not tread in the oceans of impossibility or linger where things that cannot be changed reside. They during the darkness let their lights shine.

A "Reality of Confusion" Escaping a Prison of Addiction

Throughout my career with at risk youth and even in my own life I have found that every single person in an addict's immediate family and extended family is affected by the individual's substance abuse or addiction depending on the form it takes. You see not all addictions are chemical or drug related. Those years with the youth revealed the "real life" battles of young people just like me but with a major difference. They were still Guardians of the ashes. A Reality of Confusion is that invisible battlefield where truth is distorted and obscured beneath the veil of broken hearts and dreams. It is found in the same place as that oubliette guarded by two dragons mentioned at the start of this yarn. Their names are Fear and Discouragement.

Like many with addiction, Jasmine escaped her reality through substance abuse. The victim of sexual abuse and forced prostitution by those who were supposed to love her robbed her of her own autonomy. It was something this author could partially relate to as my prison did not involve drugs but anger management and lack of self-worth. After being placed into foster care another thing I did understand, she established a drug addiction in her early teen years leading her to the facility I once worked in. She was one of so many passing through those revolving doors. Like many of the youth in that place she made a valid point as we sat in our weekly D&A group one Friday evening. She said,

"Unless you've been through addiction yourself, you'll never be able to understand what someone with an addiction is going through."

From where I sat she was not wrong.

The scars and pains left in the wake of yesterday are confronted differently by the individual facing it. I also know that addiction comes in many forms.

My cousin and I have been conversing a lot over the past year about his own struggles which he has allowed me to share. While he gave me permission to use his name I have chosen not to but share his story because it is Resiliency that broke his chains. If you are reading this and you have never struggled with an addiction, alcohol, drugs, pornography, smoking, living, social media, etc. than you do not know that addiction takes away your willingness to live a healthy and happy life.

This is what happened to Jasmine and for a time my cousin. When I asked my cousin what it was that set him on his journey and eventually imprisoned him in a "Reality of Confusion" which was the title of his own journal, he said it started at home. Before I soldier on I loved my uncle and before the end of his life he was becoming a better version of himself. Though my cousin told of how his father would drink in front of him and even offer him some at eight years of age when he first got a taste for alcohol, I found myself reminded of the transformation which had occurred. In my cousin's mind drinking was not like doing drugs so it couldn't be that bad.

At a School Picnic in the sixth-grade peer pressure would take him to a place where he never thought he would be as his older brother was into cannabis and my cousin had witnessed it. Then because his brother was like a super hero to him this façade had been created that seemed to say weed and marijuana was not same thing so he tried it at friend's house thinking if his brother did it, it will be ok. Like the many youth I once worked with the story was the same as cannabis escalated to harder drugs and a full out war with addiction was being fought. At age fifteen he started in on Cocaine and hanging with high school kids while having trouble staying in school.

For a time, I remember he came to live with us and as we have talked over the years he told me that when he had family structure things got better. He said our trip to NYC was his most memorable because we had watched Beauty and Beast on Broadway and even though he did not want to go he discovered he liked it and learned a lot with us about family. He even made honor roll where at home with lack of structure had failing grades.

During his eleventh-grade year as he was now back at home my cousin told me of how he cracked his collar bone playing football I believe and was introduced to OxyContin pain killers. It appeared his life was spiraling out of control. For one who does not understand addiction or has lived with it they will never understand. For me I never found myself in this dark place but saw the effect it had on people I knew.

One of my good friends overdosed on Heroine a week after I had talked to him. Another one of my friends who ran cross country with me died of alcohol poisoning in his college dorm. It seemed to be a vicious cycle. My cousin found himself introduced to that same drug that took the life of my friend by his girlfriend. Heroine! The part of my cousin's story that hits me the hardest is that as his father became a better version of himself and found with in him that Spirit of Resiliency and Humility he had bought for my cousin a grave plot because he feared the loss of his son to addiction. It resonates with me because my uncle is buried in that very plot. Against the odds and by the Grace of God my cousin has been free of heroine for over sixteen years now. His storms of yesterday are not his storms of today.

When I asked my cousin what it was that fueled and inspired him to escape that prison of addiction, his answer touched me deeply. The driving force behind some reasons he had turned to that lifestyle was the same one that would teach him people can change.
It was my uncle's transformation and I imagine the love of my mother playing a major role in my cousin's life. My uncle placed his faith in Christ and while he was no saint and far from perfect he knew that by Grace we are forgiven and redeemed moving him to give up drinking. He still had his struggles but now he could face each day with hope.

I believe that addiction is like a solar eclipse, for a time the moon engulfs the sun with its shadow hiding the sun but the "reality" of this confusion between light and dark has a universal truth. The sun never left because it is still there. It is identical to the eclipse I mention earlier about emotions. For the individual trapped by addiction that vice, that thing that numbs their pain does just that; but beneath the eclipse of that addiction the pain remains. Today my cousin still has battles he is fighting; but who doesn't? His life has helped me better understand the "why" things happen as they do sometimes.

It also reminds me that the Spirit of Resiliency is a powerful thing and that courage is often a measure of our self-esteem and will. Courage makes us as individuals different from others. My mother use to tell me that anything worth doing is hard. This means relationships, jobs, life in general. The drive to embrace living is illustrated on the canvas of what we believe and the influence of belief over our own individual will. It is coming to understand that we cannot do it alone and that is always "the difficult path "we must venture.

When I was on the mountain many years ago I worked and supervised the mental health unit. It was there I met a young man we will call Drake. Now this is a kid that will forever remain in my memory. He was a good kid with bad circumstances and choices. His story did not end like my cousins and I wonder sometimes "what if" he endured. Where would he be today? At thirteen, Drake was acquainted with marijuana by his father. He had also committed inappropriate acts against women which led him to Deep Run Mountain. Using marijuana eventually led to other harder drugs and it distorted Drakes mind. He was a nineteen-year-old boy with the mindset of a thirteen-year-old, perhaps that same thirteen-year-old who had danced with Mary Jane all those years before.

I can still see him talking to himself in his room after lights out and then when he thought no one was around I could hear his tears as they seemed to quietly dance of the walls. Many people believed his was crazy, other's thought he was seeking attention, but for many of us even in the worst of times, we realize that we still have things in our lives for which we are thankful and blessed. This was not the case for Drake. His father was in jail for life, his mother gone and he never said where or why. He was a nineteen-year-old kid with nowhere to go and Deep Run Mountain was his home and the staff his family. So, each time that the opportunity came to leave he would purposely sabotage it. Drake's coping mechanism other than his bizarre imagination was in his attempts to purposely have staff restrain him. It was not until I thought like him I found a solution and the first time I tried it my peers were baffled.

"Restrain me Lynch, come on little guy" he would taunt.

But Drake never fought back after being restrained. One day I said,

"Drake I am tired and do not feel good. I got an idea how about you restrain yourself and I will do the paper work for you?"

Looking at me he threw himself on the floor with his arms behind his back all while saying,

"Ok that works."

From that day at least while I was on shift Drake was never involved in a physical intervention. When he felt the need he placed himself in one. It is too bad that in his life he could not do this.

When he finally was too old to remain, he was released. I heard sometime later he was killed by a drug dealer and it broke my heart. What is reality? Is it that place between dreams and the present moment? Is it the "truth's" we tell ourselves to justify our actions. I still am not sure I can answer that. What I do know is that each person creates for themselves a reality real to them even if it is not a beneficial one for them. For many like Drake whether addiction is the chain that binds them or simply the past, reflecting on yesterday is the time to beat ourselves up for failing to endure, it is a learning moment. All the years that yesterday haunted me and even now with some storms I am facing as I write this paragraph, I have asked myself if I am good enough. Am I resilient? I want to one day look back on my life and know that my scars really to tell the stories of "*all the times life tried to knock me down but failed.*" A "Reality of Confusion" does not differ from being a Guardian of the Ashes for in that place resiliency cannot coexist with giving up.

Years ago, this Author sat in a room by his self as a troubled youth. It was while living in the group home he mentioned earlier in the Lehigh Valley. That room where I lived for almost two years was my own reality of confusion one might say. Sometimes as I stared out the window the nights when rain fell and it seemed to mask my tears. There was a longing for freedom that never seemed close by. Yet, the freedom to allow my tears to dance in cadence with the rain was the only certain form of solitude I can recall. On the other nights when the moon seemed to dance high above the world I use to believe I could chase it across the world. I came to discover once I left that place that chasing the moon is like chasing freedom to the end of a rainbow. There is no finish line because such a place does not exist inside the stained-glass landscape of worldly living. It does not differ from saying "tomorrow will be better" or "I will do this tomorrow" because tomorrow never actually comes. It will always be one step ahead of us and that is why today is so important.

A dear friend from church many years later would illustrate for me that such freedom that allows one to move forward is found inside of the human soul. Her story helped me better understand this inner freedom or as she would say thought process of being "Kingdom Minded" which allows an individual to break free from the reality of confusion they are trapped in

As illustrated in this section; this reality of confusion comes in so many forms. Everyone's storms vary but have a common thread that weaves them all together. It is the façade of a comforting inner voice which as time marches on morphs into a viscous dragon ripping apart the human soul. The voice unkindly chastises the victim for indulging in the very sinful pleasures it had once catalyzed in the forges of personal desire. In the darkness of that dungeon mentioned at the very start of this yarn those Dragons breathe words telepathically saying;

"You tweaked out junkie you will never be anything more than that. You said you were not going to drink and come home wasted anymore!"

Back and forth they hurl insults and reminders like,

"You've ruined everything. Everyone you meet you hurt! You'll always be a fat cow. You would be better off dead!" The list of shortcomings goes on.

My friend Emily found herself like so many you have met on this literary voyage trapped in that ocean known as the reality of confusion. It was how she climbed out of the grave that is a testimony to the spirit of resiliency. Through much of this journey it may seem as though there have been more tales of those who remained bound but it is in this moment, I would like to illustrate resiliency in its truest form.

My friend spent most of her life in the church, she grew up in it. I share this because so many people think that because someone believes in God that no trouble will befall them. While my friend never said that I know there are many individuals I have met who have said such things and believe those who claim to have faith should be perfect. Here is a spoiler alert that everyone probably already knows, adversity and hardship will not discriminate. It is not prejudice or care by what name you call God or if you even call him at all. Emily discovered in her youth she was living on free will.

At seventeen she lived at home and lived the life of what she thought freedom looked like. Over the next four to five years of her life she found herself in a slow fade. At first this new life seemed great until she became like one of the many youth I once worked with.

Somewhere along that highway of this new-found freedom she had engaged in drug and alcohol abuse. However, that is not where it started. If you saw my friend today you would never know that she struggled with her weight and in her life told me she weighed 225 pounds and stood at 5 feet 8 inches. This battle led to her having an eating disorder and where that slow fade perhaps began.

The aftermath of forced starvation and bulimic tendencies left Emily with stomach ulcers and other physical traumas. Still, the worst scars were received on the battlefield of her mind where memories reside. The feelings of self-worthlessness and lack of self-image continually led the assault on the way she saw herself. I have told so many young ladies this including my wife, and the ones I worked with on the mountain because I believe it to be a steadfast truth. God made women perfect, their only flaw is that they cannot see their own worth through the same lenses He does. The same can be said of men as we are all made in the image of God and loved by him.

While sharing her story with some young people Emily told of how she had this wonderful job and how the first compromises she had made was when she first tried weed and drank. If you have read closely there is a pattern. My cousin went through it and I am certain someone reading this has seen this pattern or dare I say be living it. It starts with those innocent things but then someone comes into your life like my cousin and Emily introducing you to cocaine and then even crystal meth in Emily's situation. Addiction is a thief because anyone who struggles with any addiction has reality stolen from them. They become trapped in an arena where a critical inner voice stands in judgment of them.
Emily once said that,

"After I tried those other drugs I was hook line and sinker, and it got me through each day"

She also said something that will stick with me until the day I die because there is so much validity in it.

"Everything that is fun has a price tag. You can't go to the movies, bowling or go carting without paying because all cost money. So, does sin, drinking and drug usage all have a price and one day you come to a place where you are so far in debt and cannot pay. The drugs and alcohol steals your mind and memory, that's the price you pay."

There were often during sharing her story with the young people moments she would talk of waking up covered in bruises with no memory of the night before. Emily would go days without sleep and eventually the black silhouettes of distorted memories came in waking dreams and lucid hallucinations. Truly Emily was trapped in a reality of confusion. Her world had become small and she stood at the edge of it, looking into that dark abyss. One night would become the catalyst which would change all that. What started off as fun and enjoyable reached a point where Emily said,

"There is no way out of this; I am never going to be anyone so the only way out is death"

Those are such chilling words and to the point of utter hopelessness. It is the very intersection mentioned often in this narrative that changes the trajectory of the human condition and temperature of the soul. One night she sat alone in her apartment overdosing on meth when she lay on floor. Looking over to the mirror on the wall she saw the distorted reflection of the person she had become. Somehow, she crawled over to that mirror. Sitting against it she thought in that moment she was about to die. As she starred into that mirror, that gateway to a reversed reflection all she could think of was that little girl who loved Jesus and Sunday school so much as she rocked back and forth sobbing. She told me sitting there that as she looked in the glass she kept saying repeatedly,

"Who are you, who are you?"

Something changed that night and since my friend shared this story with me it is evident she did not die. In oceans where many weary travels drown she was close to giving up and ready to die. The road ahead was still filled with pot holes and rough terrain. Addiction's gravity is strong like the force from Star Wars and can pull you back in quickly. Like that unsuspecting under toe that finds you one minute on the shore and the next second in the depths of an unforgiving ocean it can suck you back out to sea.

Though her mother pushed her into a much-needed intervention she found herself checked in to the New Life for Girls rehab facility which was a biblically based facility. Emily was the only girl there who had not been to jail though she knew often it was the Grip of Grace which kept her from it. All the other girls there were court ordered. It was not long before she left and though she had clean, addiction's under-toe pulled back into that abyss.

The final straw would be day her husband/boyfriend at the time came home and found her crack pipe. He had bared witness to the devastation and brokenness left in the wake of drug abuse inside the concreate corridors of his past from those close to him. The look on his face revealed anger, hurt but most of all because he loved her so much, disappointment. He ran outside and smashed that crack pipe on the ground. Emily had become so tired of hurting everyone and ruining every positive relationship.

How than did my friend climb out of the grave? How did she once and for all escape that reality of confusion? You see like all the individuals in this yarn she was constantly trying to fix herself and redeem herself to others which is exhausting and impossible. It is not something that can be done in one's own power. Therefore; while much of Emily's story has seemed to center on that mind made prison our journey now takes us from the grave to new life through a *"renewing of the mind"*.

Addiction no matter what it is can be the worst bondage because the prisoner feels like there is no way out but there is! She remembered that little girl who did love Jesus and Sunday school and she knew that she needed to surrender her burdens and allow him to carry her cross. Romans 3:26 echoed through her mind as she realized that God knew before we were even thought of we would compare sin with pleasure and fun. *"For the wages of sin is death"* the author of Romans had written many years ago. God also knew we would pay a price for our fun, for the comforting inner voices which led us astray. My friend was right *"everything comes at a price."*

After she had married her husband whom I am also becoming close to, the birth of her first daughter and one of five children, confirmed for her that life had begun to change. She wanted to be the best mother she could and her daughter saved her life. It was the "defining moment" she would step out of the ashes and become a Keeper of the Flame.

Now this Author has said it before and will say it again. This yarn is not about conversion of faith. It is at times about those who placed their hope in a Savior they could not see but knew to be as real as that summer breeze I mentioned from my Army days. Should the reader feel inspired to question *"what if"* and then question the possibility of what the world and some scientist say is impossible fire away as it might change your life. There is nothing really to lose. Everything comes at a price, even change. Therefore; to escape any reality of confusion we must change the way we think because our thoughts are the puppeteers to our actions. For Emily she became Kingdom Minded transforming her thoughts to align with the Jesus she loved so much. Inside the Art Gallery of her mind she had removed and burned all the dark paintings once stored there and replaced them with Precious Art that Jesus Christ himself would look at and smile because of them.

This Author found for him that the real enemy was not so much the past or the things he did wrong. Rather I marvel upon the idea that if the reality of confusion we find ourselves in is our own ego which is the mere reflection of our self-image; than our mind sets need to be taken through a mental revolution to be set free. Perhaps my aim while telling and sharing these stories is to elicit the possibility that the past, the addictions, the hurt or the loss cannot be allowed to become our identity. This is easier said than done I know. Still, maybe understanding how to let go of something or someone is best illustrated through that saying, *"The darkest hour is just before the dawn."*

A Post Card from Fort Benning

Much of what has been chronicled with in the fabric of these pages has been a look at so many lives which once collided with my own. Many might say that within the vast ocean of these memories there has been more sadness then hope and so for a moment I would like to share one flash in a time not forgotten because of the hope it brought.

December had the breath of new snow, but this December would bring a gift unlike any I had received. In the wake of remembering my mother's words about the realism of change in one's heart because the idea was planted by someone who cared enough to soldier on even when everyone else gave up; I received a post card from Fort Benning Georgia while I still worked on the Mountain. Inside were two pictures of the same person. One was a teen whose hair was braided and whose skin allowed piercings to be visible. Upon his face a stern and sad like look. His eyes hinted of shame and confusion a lot like my own years before. His body art illustrated the neighborhood he was from and was a reminder of another place and time.

The other photo showed that same kid no longer a troubled youth from the City of Brotherly Love but rather; a man! The man smiling slightly a smile of pride and his eyes beamed with accomplishment. This man was dressed from head to toe in his Army Dress Greens, hair well-kept and styled into a fade that now revealed an American soldier.

On the back of the post card were written the words,

"Mr. Lynch I kept my promise and thank you for believing in me!!!"

I smiled and showed my boss and friend Tyler what I had received as a tear snuck from the corner of my eye and the feeling of guilt came over me. Deep down I had not believed in this city kid from the other side of the tracks and the thought of it perforated my gut.

"Way to go Antonio" I whispered, *"way to go."*

It was I think in that moment my faith had been restored a bit. All the death, the revolving door that welcomed repeated offenders and statistics that seemed to ring true for a moment were replaced with hope.

Antonio Rivera grew up headed straight for a life of violence and the short life expectancy of a gang member. He had no cause other than to survive. Antonio was the son of immigrant parents and he was the first generation born in the United States. "Toni" as everyone called him grew up in a neighborhood where the only people to look up to were involved in violent cliques, drug deals and death. He was first arrested in the fifth grade, while he spent his time hanging around older kids. Toni struggled in school and was kicked out of high school his junior year. Looking around at the wreckage of gang involvement and the deaths of close friends and family, Antonio made a monumental choice. He worked with kids who inspired him to reach for a better life.

These days he still serves his country but as one who can look back through faded years and offer the hope of what is possible when change is embraced. Is that not the Spirit of Resiliency? To come out of darkness where light overtakes it with the influence of hope and is inspired by the dreams men and women dare to dream even when they began as nightmares. Is that not the Spirt of Resiliency reminding others it can be done? Another year was almost over, and a fresh, new one was just around the corner. The past for Antonio was behind him now, and with it went the victories and trials, the mistakes and its newly adopted understandings. There was a hope for tomorrow and the once broken city kid had become a man.

Antonio reminded me that while many things are uncertain in life this steadfast truth is universal: Each one of us has a past, it's defining moments and foundations regardless of how stable the pillars of what makes a person who they are. That past in which the Guardian once stood watch is now only there to remind us from where we came but not where we have remained. The unreachable dimension of Yesteryear now out of our grasp is there now only to instruct and inform but it does not need to define us. It is an individual alone with the power to do that through the Spirit of Resiliency like that river I have mentioned often before because I believe it to be true that is always flowing forward, never moving back or standing still. In doing this we must step out of our comfort zones and comfort zones are not really about comfort, they are about overcoming fear. I have discovered that jumping into deep waters with hope breaks the chains of fear and leaves them in the sand where we once walked and left our footprints.

Chains in the Sand

When I was a soldier I never found myself in some far away jungle or dessert. I did not see men fall before me on a bloody battlefield or lose a friend as many brave men and women have done for this country. Still Life is a battlefield all of its's own. The War has no name it just is. There on that field where Yesterday positions His Howitzers, Regret and Sorrow place themselves on either side of our soul preparing to flank us when the hour seems darkest. When the daily battle begins deep inside of our mind's eye; yesterday fires from His Howitzer's the memories which chain us in the Dessert Sand of hopelessness. It is a hot desolate place which exists only in the mind of the soldier fighting his or her own internal war. Woven throughout this tome you have read about what it means to be "A Guardian of the Ashes." You walked with those who sank in the quick sand of the past and you have read of those who "Stepped out of the Ashes." So, then what does it mean to become "A Keeper of the Flame"? Are you someone chained to your past? In every life, regardless of its background or origin we so often find ourselves on that vast battlefield of life mentioned earlier.

The lobes of our souls listen to the linguistic melodies of our imperfections and bad choices and we far too often feel as though we will not rise from the fall. The Keeper of the Flame chooses to rise out of the darkness they are in. They leave in the sand those chains that bound them. It is hard for sure, but it is in changing the way we think that changes the way we feel and act. My entire life, I have cried out often through my behavior as the bullets of regret, hurt, abuse and sin pierced my spiritual flesh. Before I dared to place my hope and faith in a God I could only see through the world around me and the blessings with in my life; I was dying. The things that scarred us I have cultured become the stories we tell others. They remind us that what we have done, or what has been done to us, need not define who we will become. In understanding this one can look back and see those "Chains in the Sand."

Every life and every story inside of these pages have been the stories of real people. You might have even seen yourself through one of them or you know someone whose life unfolded before your eyes while reading. Not everyone believes as I do and that is ok. I can only share how God has allowed me to become a Keeper of the Flame even when the flame burns dim. Just because a person places there trust in God, it does not mean the war ends. It rages harder and harder. The difference is through the smoke and fire the soldier will endure even when it feels like the world is falling apart. Even if everything will not "be ok." Tell no one it will be ok, because we do not know for sure. The best thing anyone ever said was "nothing" if there were no words to say. The fact that they were there for me said everything

Regardless; of what philosophers and the "politically correct" might say, Life is an arena painted red with sin, sorrow and hope because we must battle the forces of the lower self and negative ego within and without. Everyday regardless of our past we must encounter our own negative characteristics, destructive thoughts, feelings, emotions and verves whispered into our lives by one who opposes God because he fell from the stars beyond paradise. Therefore; life is a battlefield where every day is a battle to save souls and heal the fallen and brokenhearted. However; even as we are at war with ourselves I have learned this truth and have sealed it in the deepest parts of my soul because it gives me strength when I am at my weakest.

It reminds me to look back and see the Chains in the Sand. I now know and believe that God's heart breaks when Yesterday's sorrow and loss robs us of our hopes and dreams. It reminds me he is going through the storm with me even when I cannot see him and that I am not alone. When the battle becomes fierce and the word's *"you're not good enough"* bounce off the walls of my soul and return like before, I remember that my real value and worth the uniqueness I have as a child of God drives me onward and out of the darkness.

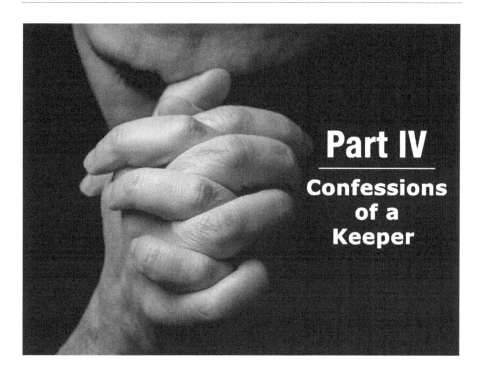

Part IV

Confessions of a Keeper

Illusions of Tomorrow

The only thing in my life I can now be certain of is change. Even more so when embraced and guided by God's Grace and Mercy is it beneficial. This very narrative which chronicles Guardians of the Ashes, those who dared to step out and those who became Keepers of the Flames, speaks of change and how like a river it is moving with or without us. In telling my story and the stories of others the illusions of tomorrow along with the brokenness of days now past no longer hold me because everything changes, from the moment we're born to the moment we die. It is in the reality of enduring that we find life has many twists and turns, and our insight of what reality is or is not shapes us to become who we are. More importantly how we feel does not mean it is the absolute truth. Feelings come and go but truth will always be truth.

The biggest issue in living I feel; is that like me so many people trapped in the past we spend too much time on what was that we do not see today and all its intricate possibilities. The Illusions of Tomorrow, wasted memories and time I have spent deciphering the difference between reality and that which was not reality; once kept me bound as it does so many others and perhaps even someone reading this right now. What makes letting go so hard? How does one look beyond where they were to focus on now? Furthermore; how does one even define reality? For me as I said before, I once escaped into stories of myth and music from another place and time and called it reality but my reality, my illusions of tomorrow were fantasies. Reality is so hard to explain because it is unique to everyone. However; I would submit to the fact that reality in the sense I am trying to drive the point home is the foundation of what is true and what is not. The force that keeps us in the past or allows us to flow forward like that river.

Life has led me to believe that our environment and the people we are around shape our perception of what is real but that does not mean it is. Realism is our grip of what is true and false, right and wrong, what is real and what is not. So, reality can and is often distorted by our belief in it. We can sincerely believe something is right, but be sincerely wrong. I know I have. By this understanding I go back to a simple solution. However, it is easier said than done. I know this to be true. To change one's actions, they must change the way they think. There is no illusion in that.

This may be another spoiler alert for much of the world but escape from hardships in the future and in life is impossible. It comes to us all but the key to getting through it and I mean getting through it is we must keep nothing for tomorrow. If life is a journey, sure, we should have a target for tomorrow, the memories of yesterday and the experiences of this moment but we must not wait for it to come. The many "figurative moments" and those "defining" ones instilled in me the certainty that the phrase "Tomorrow never comes" is a universal truth because when it arrives at our door step it becomes today. This Author believes that *"Tomorrow will never come"* is whispered of a tomorrow when excited for it to arrive and the wait seems to take forever. The reason I wish to drive this point home is that I believe that Tomorrow never comes is an expression which signifies the importance of today. Whatever changes you are longlining to make begin doing it Today.

Penning this manuscript has been a reminder that the stories we tell ourselves cause us the most suffering and courage to move onward into the present moment. It is not usually situations necessarily good or bad per se, but the stories we tell ourselves about them and the judgement we create. Again, it is the way we think of life and the world. My biggest problem when letting the past go, was that I had convinced myself those things, the memories and mistakes just were what they were. I was actively and un-intentionally limiting myself to living within the constraints of a small box suffocating me and robbing me of joy. It is no different I suppose than getting into a car with no steering wheel; death whether physical or emotional is imminent. More so, that revelation that one cannot truly "let go" only move on has now remained etched in my mind.

We all have issues and situations in life, and no matter how good someone else's life may appear, the grass is not always greener on the side. This is but another Illusion of Tomorrow. Often, I found those other lives didn't have grass, but synthetic plastic. My mother taught me we all have different talents and gifts and not to envy those of others, but to appreciate and value my own. It's through our various gifts that make us members of the one body of Christ. (Corinthians 1:12) Surround yourself with people aware of your greatness. Believe that through Christ all things are possible and let your faith anchor you in that steadfast truth.

I have met so many people that do not understand that Time, as we know it, is only an illusion. Past, Present, Future is the scale upon which we measure our existence. Yet, if they could see as I did almost too late, the Past, yesterday is only a collection of memories. While in those moments when all seemed to go wrong cut us deepest the present offers an unrecognizable gift. We cannot experience the Past, we can only remember it. That is a choice everyone makes. The funny thing is we can remember it only in the Present suggesting that our memories are noticeably unreliable. In my own life there have been moment's where I have tried to fill in gaps posing the question was it that bad, or perhaps it was worse and God's Grace has kept that from me.

Over the years which have swiftly morphed into decades I now understand that to move beyond what I could not change I had believe that to "Be Here Now" was not just good advice in some self-help book. Rather; it's the only possibility. This crazy dreamer of a Writer learned that If we want to experience the deepest truth of things as they are, we must be in harmony with being here, now. We cannot do that on our own. With this thought I must make another confession. It is only in Christ alone that we can find the deepest truth of things as they are. Truth is a universal understanding we all seek to know and recognize.

Throughout God's word the importance of speaking the truth is habitually woven throughout the fabric of the greatest story ever penned in Truth and the breath of God himself. John 16:13 outlines clearly, how such harmony is obtained. It does not mean the road is easy. I will never tell anyone it is! It just means that as change comes we endure through it and find joy in our suffering and happiness. *"But when he, the Spirit of truth, comes, he will guide you into all the truth. He will not speak on his own; he will speak only what he hears, and he will tell you what is yet to come."*

"Man, in the Mirror"

Everyone I am sure has heard the song. They may have even danced to it, or become emotional while watching the music video. Yet, do they grasp in their mind's eye the power behind those lyrics made famous by the King of Pop Michael Jackson?

"I'm gonna make a change, for once I'm my life, it's gonna feel real good, Gonna make a difference Gonna make it right."

To overcome and face each present day, the truth I have discovered is that we must want to and to do that we must face our greatest enemy, ourselves. For so many years I hated myself for things I had done. Even as I am placing my thoughts on to my keyboard in my present moment which will be my past your present once you have read it; I find images of the greatest storm I have ever faced in my life taunting me and calling me a hypocrite. While I am still trying to make sense of it and understand the "why" I am left baffled. Yet, all that God has brought me through reminds me that even if the outcome is not what I imagined, it will be ok if I will take my own words which I have penned and apply them to myself in this moment, this current storm I am in.

On this Ocean we call life we come to find that if we never are in a storm, we cannot become master sailors. We need those storms to learn from. Life, whether good or bad is about moments and interactions. There is no way around it. Those interactions influence us and yet when I look at myself in the mirror before going to work, I have found myself wiser now believing that introspection or looking inside ourselves regardless of what we might find is an opportunity to become a better version of ourselves. Unfortunately I have also noticed in that mirror four distinct grey hairs in my goatee reminding me that time is flying by.

Introspection, if one is willing serves as the telescope into our souls. Through that crystal scope we see more deeply into who we are and who we long to be. At least that's what I see. Sometimes it is not comfortable because while we can con the world we cannot cheat ourselves from the truth or the One in whose *"image we were fearfully and wonderfully made."* Psalms 139:14

Many people have asked me to include some close to me why I have written about all that you have read and I think I now know for certain the "why". When I started I was not sure as it was just a feeling that seemed to evolve into a hope that just maybe my life could be a living breathing example of what Grace and Mercy looks like. An example of what weakness looks like and that it is ok to be weak for through our weakness God reveals himself and the power he wields. While that remains some of the reason, I imagine as this will be my last book on the subject it has been to offer hope to others while closing a large chapter in my own life. Over the years I have said I have forgiven others and yet my mom was right, there has been much I did not let go until recently and I can see it in the pages I have fashioned. I am not ashamed of that because it has taught me that moving forward and choosing to "make it right" begins with the man in the mirror.

Much of my life my innermost thoughts, the ones no one else knows about; whether they were fashioned from my own mind's eye or cultured from others have shaped my life. The interesting thing is that all the lives which have intersected with mine and even the unknown reader who has come this far with me, share this universal trait, whether they want to admit or not. For anyone longing to live a life worth living they must begin with introspection. It is when refusal to accept change begins with the way the reflection in the mirror reveals shades of hopelessness and lack of self-worth and value. Bruce Lee whether you like him or not was a good philosopher and said it best. If I have quoted him on this before I am sorry but I feel it is appropriate here. *"A man walking in darkness will never find the light until he realizes he is walking in darkness."*

Millions of Ships on Troubled Waters

As the accounts with in this narrative come to its close it is important that to emphasize an imperative and essential fact. My story as I have shared it and all those lives which have collided with mine are now in your past because you have journeyed with me this far. On the flip side of that coin, for me right now you are with me in my present as these words and thoughts unfold randomly it seems but still with a vivid recollection of years gone by. I imagine we are all time travelers through written memories but I cannot leave you here without a few more confessions which I must make.

Throughout my life so many people have asked me how I could heal from being shipwrecked on Life's Island of Broken Dreams as I mentioned earlier I believe with Calvin. So, this is my first confession. While this narrative, every person even if names were altered, every circumstance and every encounter were as real as the sunrise and sunset. Throughout the journey in which you have been a part of I clarified that this story was not written to convert or sway anyone to my beliefs and values and to this my stand remains unchanging as when I began. However, as I relived these moments I was also reminded that I never said I would not tell my readers what God has done in my life and what it was that has led me to the steadfast belief that His hands have brought me to this moment in time. For me to deny that the whispers of His voice have placed into my mind a way to tell a story true to every walk of life regardless of where they are would be an unforgivable sin against Him.

For this Author it sincerely has been through the belief in Jesus Christ he dares to imagine that he has been redeemed and transformed into a child of God. This dreamer of impossible dreams has become like "a phoenix rising from the ashes" as a new creation because his mind had been renewed and way of thinking changed. I recall before believing in this steadfast truth wondering why I had been taken into such troubled waters. I did not realize that it was because in that place my enemies could not swim but God's hands would keep me from drowning.

I look at it this way; if I dare to believe in something I cannot see I lose nothing. Like the beliefs of so many I am just dead when I leave this world and nothing more but ash and dust. Yet; if I choose not to believe what the universe has shown me to be true time and time again in my life through unexplainable moments where the impossible was possible; then I will lose my very soul which will remain long after this mortal coil has returned to the earth from which it came. I wonder for those reading who might not have thought of who God is in this way; could they find it possible to imagine they have nothing to lose by believing He created them for something spectacular in a world where the impossible places limits on our fragile human minds?

I do not intend to preach as I am a writer of what I know from experience and have endured. I weave my personal conclusions and values within the fabric of that beautifully interlaced quilt of how darkness was over taken by light. Every journey is different, each person and circumstance diverse and unique. Our ideals and philosophies etched on the canvas of our past, present and uncertain futures help to fashion and cultivate those truths. Still, there to be a universal Truth that saved my life all those years ago and His name was Jesus Christ. Upon belief I can only say with a resolute assurance guided by my faith, God Just Is! It is because of the hardships I can tell others of who God is and how He has worked so diligently in my life molding me into the man I have become. The man many have asked how he overcame. I still struggle everyday but I am no longer without hope. Even when there have been days that have tried my soul especially in my most recent battle I cry out and praising God for what he has done for me.

You see; God repeatedly has given glimpses of who He is through His written word which I cannot stress enough! I promise you it is not just another book or set of rules. It is a story of what love is. Until recently I did not swim in that ocean as often has I should of. It has been one of my many character flaws which I am trying every day to correct. I know too many people especially those suffering, to them it is another book a lot like those stories I use to read of Demi God's and Goddess's. Yet; beyond all of that, I have felt God's Grace in my life and that is not something I can explain. My transformation from Guardian of the Ashes to Keeper of the Flame began when I sought after Him and thirsted to know Him believing He would not hide from me even in those deep waters I was in. I believed with an assurance I cannot describe that He longed for me to love and trust Him even if I could not see him. I believe we were created. To love and be loved, and to worship Him and call Him father.

There are millions and millions of ships on that ocean of life. As they are tossed and battered I know they are longing for truth, something to believe in that is real. I know because I like them was pushed away by other ships who claimed to be Christian and yet the nature of their lives contradicted the life that seemed worth living. The glimpses of judgment and stereotypical individuals hindered me at one point. That troubled water will never let up even if we trust in the creator of heaven and earth. I found it got tougher and the storms raged more fiercely as I might have mentioned before. For me it was the faith that when those days came where I passed through troubled waters, I could hear beneath the storm God's voice saying,

"I will be with you; and when you pass through the rivers, they will not sweep over you. When you walk through the fire, you will not be burned; the flames will not set you ablaze." -Isaiah 43:2

I know many people even my friends reading this out of support for my writing and storytelling, do not believe God exists. For some it is the illustrations of their sorrow and suffering that causes them to question and doubt that a loving God could look down from his throne and not touch them in a special way. However, I know he came down from his throne to where the people were and touched them. One friend currently an Agnostic but searching pulled me aside one night after a long shift with troubled teens and asked,

"do you think I will ever find this God that saved you? I mean Clayton how do you work in such darkness and still are able to smile at those who curse at you and spit on you? You are different."

Wow…. what a question. How does one answer that? Especially when you know you battle darkness every day. I thought for a moment as I do not want to ever become a "bible beater for Jesus" but rather a witness for Jesus. I want to allow God to work through me and I figured my friend asked me for a reason, he could have asked anyone. I recall saying,

"I imagine it is up to you but even if you don't find him, I believe and am faithful He will find you."

I thought about that night a lot and often since, even though my own search for God was hardly intense because I thought I was right with him. However, as I grew older and wiser I began banging my heart against the Golden gates of heaven because I knew that I along with humanity was created for so much more than what I was offering. I had to stop trying to be someone I was not and be who God made me to be. I will honestly say I still am not sure I know, but I pray one day I will. There on the Mountain Top of Introspection I saw the defining moment when I was "figuratively tapped on the shoulder" by God's Holy Spirit and first believed. It was that summer at camp I mentioned earlier in these pages and there was something the evangelist had said that day I knelt at that alter.

'It is an undeniable sadness to go through life without loving or being loved" he said in his enchanting British accent.

I now am certain it is those memories that along with so many others that moved me to pen this book; because love I have cultivated is a choice carried out daily on the wings of Grace and Mercy regardless of how often or by whom I have been wronged. The feeling of love fades like a campfire greeted by the following morning but the love that changes the world is an act. It is keeping no records of those who have wronged us even when the wrong has left scars that no one else can see. Jesus demonstrated it perfectly. He died for those who loved him and those who never will. That has taught me that loving others means sometimes loving those who will never love me. Believe me even as a believer rereading my own words there is that part of me saying,

"Uh…. really"?

Then I hear a whisper inside of me say,

"yes really."

That type of love is an Agape love an until recent events unfolded in my life I did not know what that was. In layman's terms and no fancy metaphors or symbolism Agape simply put is unconditional love! It is the hardest type of love to give others but it has been given to us.

I hope that you will not abandon ship here because of my confession. The ability to place words into motion I realize does not come from me anymore or anything I have done. What I am certain of is that the millions of ships on the troubled waters of life if filled with the Spirit of Resiliency will discover that regardless of yesterday our lives are not ended because of an earthly death, only changed. The courage it takes to not only find shelter in the storm but to then go back out and help others do the same requires a prodigious metamorphosis from a dream into Faith unshaken. That Spirit of Resiliency that gives one the fortitude and bravery to face that ocean each day, is to discover a life though imperfect, is far more beautiful than the Eye of Humanity or even the Human Condition itself has ever seen or the mind ever dare to imagine.

The Lighthouse in the Storm

Every now and then when I am tempted with treading once more in the oceans of the past I ask God's forgiveness for my sins every day. I ask him to place in my mind's eye the blessings I sometimes over look in the crowded streets of day to day living. It is the Light House in the present storm I am facing that guides me back to where I know I am supposed to be. Here is another confession and it is not much of one but more of a fact. So many people think that just because I go to church, believe in God, speak at different events, and treat people the best I can, that I have it all together. If only you could see into the mindscape of this Writers thoughts. I will never have it all together. None of us ever will. There will many more days when Life's dark skies look like ink spilled from its bottle onto the pages of our lives.

So, it is that when I have my face on the floor praying for forgiveness for my thoughts regardless of if I have acted upon them, I'm faced with a hardcore truth. I, too, am called to forgive others. I mean forgive them. How do you know when you have done that? I took until the age of maybe thirty-four to forgive my biological mother. I mean I told the world and God I had but really, I carried it with me years into my adulthood. Through writing this book I discovered I had not done this and this book has been six years now in the making. It is likely the reason thoughts may appear in random order and yet still weave together a linguistic medley of resiliency. It was a question that my mother asked me when she wanted to know why I was still writing about my child-hood. I recall responding with because it is what I know, it is a chapter in my life that has helped to fashion the story of my life.

This is why this will be my final writing on my own life. It was that Light House, God's touching of my heart I prayed that my biological mother discovered who He was so I could see her one day in Heaven. When I saw her, I would say nothing only hug her because she would already know without a word being spoken that I forgave her. I think that when your heart can feel that way and will keep no record of the wrongs inflicted to remind the perpetrator of what they had done, you have forgiven. Grace, the light house and the Guardian Angel of Life's Darkest night allows us to move forward from this moment we were trapped in. I often wonder how long the list would be if everyone I have ever wronged was flashed before my eyes. I am certain it would stretch across America at least three-thousand miles long.

Even by reading all that has unfolded within these pages some of you might have been moved and inspired but your resolve remains regarding letting go of yesterday and stepping out of the ashes to become a Keeper of the Flame for others to come after you. Therefore; when I am broken, battered, drained I cling to this promise. It is for me The Ultimate Light House in The Storm. I pray it brings the same to you. Isaiah 43:18-19 whispers into my weariness,

"Forget what happened long ago! Don't think about the past. I am creating something new. There it is! Do you see it? I have put roads in deserts, streams in thirsty lands."

It is in these written thoughts I hope I answered my mother's question and it brought her a sense of joy.

Gravity, Wind and Oxygen

Some years ago, someone once asked me to define Faith. As I have grown in my own I have known so many people who would throw scripture at me hurling it like it was a cannon ball on fire, but while I believe in the word of God it was the simpler but thought-provoking illustrations people of great faith provided me with through their actions that influenced my heart.

I do not recall where I was in my life but I think it might have been while I was still working on the mountain. The only way I could paint a clear picture for them was like this and I am hopeful you will follow me here and ponder this for yourself as perhaps it will linger in your own mind long after these pages becomes your past. Gravity, Wind and Oxygen all have two things in common. First, they are invisible. Second, they exist and are as real as you and me. We know these things to be actual because with gravity what goes up returns to the ground and we see and feel those effects.

The wind I referenced before I believe. The language of the trees as they sway and speak to one another on a breezy day or that much needed kiss of temporary comfort on ones back on a hot summers afternoon reveals the winds presence both in seeing its effects and feeling its presence.

With each breath we take as our lungs fill up with air and we are reminded of the reality that is oxygen. So, what then is Faith? I have found it does not differ from these three Gravity, Wind and Oxygen. Think about it. In the sense I am referring to, faith believes that the universe is not infinite but was created by an infinite creator all present with in the universe. I have never nor will I ever claim to have seen the face of God, but the very storms in which I have chronicled for you with in these pages is a reminder of all the times I felt like wind; his presence in my life. I suppose this confession I am making is that as I believe I referred to before, *"Hope is the ability to hear the music of the future and Faith is the courage it takes to dance to it today."*

Through the black and white lenses of these thoughts I have visited and I have openly shared with you it was by Faith, I stepped out of my circumstances as have so many others before me. The same way many others right now in this present moment are doing in other parts of the world. It is a rare thing because humanity is driven by what their own two eyes can see that so often they do not feel what they cannot see but it still exists. Through such faith I can tell what God has done in my life. He rescued me time and time again beginning in that rickety old trailer nestled in the woods by the railroad tracks.

The Modality behind the Words

When this Author started writing down these thoughts I was praying about the different issues tackled in these pages. Who would want to read about some abused kid getting into trouble. Who would even care and would it matter anyway. Yes, I wanted to share my love for Jesus Christ but in a way that even the sceptic would apricate because the outcomes of our lives are proof of what we believe and often words are not as important. Do they have influence? They do because once spoken they cannot be retracted. I used to tell the troubled teens this story which illustrates the power words have.

There was a renowned food critic, who goes to a fancy restaurant and says to the chef,

"I want your best dish."

The chef comes back about a half hour later and places a beautiful dish in front of the critic. The critic takes a bite and exclaims,

"this is divine. What is it?"

The chef replies,

"tongue it is a rare delicacy."

So, then the critic says,

"bring me your worst dish."

The chef returns and places the dish in front of the critic within minutes. The critic takes a bite and immediately spits it out.

"My dear chef what was that it was awful."

In reply the chef says,

"It was tongue."

The point behind that anecdote was that what we say can be good or bad and can have two very different tastes. It has the power to restore or destroy. There is a saying that no one will care about our words and that they are only important to the one saying them or writing them. For an author this is a battle but not out in left field. The choices we make and actions we take validate or discredit our words. So, while words are powerful it does not compare next to that which we do.

I realized and accepting there may be many who might be offended by my observations and faith based references which I have made. Yet; I suppose if my readers found offense they would not have dared to soldier this far with me. At any rate, as a Keeper of the Flame I no longer worry what others will think about me or I would be writing to you as a hypocrite. By reflecting on my own personal life now that I have grown and that of our human culture; I find in admitting that I was one of those Guardians of the Ashes I now try to inspire with God's help, I am living proof that a life can change if we will change the way we think.

The modality, the focus behind all you have shared with me as you trekked through these pages has been to encourage and influence you because no one can make another person change. It is against the laws of human ecology and nature to change the hearts of men. Change begins with the individual. Remember that special number? One! The hardest thing throughout not only telling and sharing these memories is, loving even those who I know will never love me. Some have appeared with in this narrative. Yet, it is that Spirit of Resiliency that has enabled me to choose love enough to become a living open book.

Threshold Where Dreams Take Flight

Somewhere within the Emerald Halls of humanities' aspirations and visions there is a place we forget about when Time's hands have choked us, worn us down or life has bombarded us with shape shards of adversity. For some they never even know it exists because they remain prisoner to the past. It is the threshold where dreams take flight upon the wings of hopes and ideas of a better life. I do not speak of unrealistic dreams like those of my own youth but ones that would tell of better days. Not perfect ones, but better ones. Ask you self this, what can tomorrow bring if I would leave yesterday where it is? It is not as easy as it seems I know but in those halls the Spirit of Resiliency moves us to dream of such days.

I have discovered these days we live in a culture of entitlement and chasing more, bigger and better things, and wanting it now. Yet they are things that lose value through the years. It seems egotistical to dream people might say. However, I am not speaking of worldly things that will fade away like my very flesh will when it returns to the earth. The dreams I speak of are those that bring peace to the weary and worn down, healing to the broken and wounded. I also believe that it is ok to be chasing a dream that might be physical if one realizes that it isn't a flyby night feat. It's more of a lifestyle shift; a commitment to your unlimited potential. It does not differ from realizing the dream of eternity is truly a reality. Dream of those things and move toward them!

On that horizon where the dreamer dares to dream of impossible things this life has taught me that sometimes God uses those to not only touch the dreamer but those whose lives the dreamer intersects with. I once dreamed of being a Wordsmith and an illustrator whose rhymes and stories could touch the hearts of my readers. The Spirit of Resiliency and chasing a dream differs from being an ideological drifter in the oceans of compromise. It is seeing the images of a new beginning and striving to make it transpire with in the fabric of letting go of the past. The threshold in which I speak where dreams takes flight is an act of faith and often that means you cannot see what is ahead. Emerson said it best and it is in his words you find that threshold of where dreams take flight is true. He said,

"What lies behind us and what lies before us are tiny matters compared to what lies within us".

I hear those words often when I think now of that light with in me that once could not be felt or seen. The sorrow of years long past and the uncertainty of tomorrow fade into trivial whispers I barely hear because of the Spirit that lives in with in me. Like a river it is always moving and it is ever flowing through me.

A Writers Dream Etched in New Color

Many years ago, perhaps in middle school maybe high school I pretended to take notes on The Revolutionary War. We were talking about the Minute Men I think and their role in that war. However; all I could see during that History class was my own. I watched my hand moving across my D.C comic notebook much like I am watching the words right now appear in front of me on my computer. I noticed something strange. With a trivial, somewhat cataleptic movement of my pencil, it seemed enchanted by my mind's eye. People, places, shapes, and ideas were coming to life. The memories of yesterday and moments once true in my life were bleeding forth from my pencil as they aroused images in my head filled with meaning, emotion, and wonder as to how this was happening. I let my hand move freely as my number 2 pencil placed on that page images reborn from the black and white of my past into color filling my imagination. If you have followed me this far you might agree this was no small thing. It became a big part of who I am.

This was something unbelievable that I'd simply paid no attention to and never dreamed it would help anyone else. The most significant thing I realized was that I was not simply spelling words. Well in another time when I could spell well. You see, I was doing something wonderful even if I did not understand the gravity of it. At least in my own mind I believed this to be true. I was casting linguistic literary spells. It was another escape much like those days when I longed to live with Demi God's and Goddesses, but this, this was different because it was real.

The very reason I can share these accounts with you which lie in the oceans of a life lived through adversity and resiliency is because every line, every person you have met has been a part of my life. Foolish? Perhaps, but this is only if one underestimates the illustrations of words themselves. While I have said actions define us, the strength of words if they bare meaning and truth woven together by strands of imagination; while they cannot change the hearts of men; they can influence the heart of anyone who reads them. That is my next confession. I am striving to influence hope found through what Christ has done for me and so many others I have known. It is the gift to wield that poetic essence and recognize that they have value that *"makes all the difference."* Think about it honestly as you have read this narrative. Has your heart at any moment beat faster, or slower? Has it made you perspire in emotion you did not know you had? Has it made you cry, laugh or believe in something you once deemed impossible?

Ponder this thought if you will, that words evoke change and even deep reflection and are of the mystic type, other-worldly, and gifted to us by the Holy Spirit providing a way of shaping and molding our world and each other. Even so our lives and our experiences give us a common ground in which we can empathize with our fellow man, but are still fashioned by our own creativity, internal passions and energy at times. As sure as the sun will rise in the east and set in the west the Holy Spirit is working in someone's life right now who has been reading through these pages. Some I am sure are and will always be skeptical. Still, one can explain words and they can explain magic, but just because an explanation can be given on the impossibility that such a Truth is evident; the accounts of those who have lived the impossible illustrate the possibility of what is possible when Christ is in them. That's because humanity is driven by individual truth and misguided by humanistic belief. Across the landscape of humanity, our acceptance and understanding are not bound by logic, but by emotions.

As I said before, I may not see the wind but I feel it when it kisses my shoulders on a hot summers day. It is there invisible to the naked eye but its presence is known by the way it makes you feel. Many believe in words, the poet or storyteller breathes life into them, we toss them into the world and they thrive. Yet; before any of us ever did that or knew we could, the story of life was already being written. Like our words built upon the ideas we fashion in or head or moments we have lived; the manner and morality of our thinking not only dictate the words but more essentially the actions. To change the way, one lives they must first change the way they think.

This crazy dreamer of an Author, had to understand that he still needed to see the world as others do, while not conforming to it and often that means walking against a crowd. My son loves to write and I imagine I will always be a writer of dreams and still a dreamer of dreams too. It is what I hope for Isaiah as he discovers his creative ability built on the experiences he has yet to have. Hopefully much happier ones then many of those penned here. The black and white I knew I leave there, no longer a Guardian of the past or Sentry of broken dreams, but a writer of dreams etched in new color that is the hope of what I cannot see but can feel.

I think that when we never begin, or when we stop, when we abandon possibility, regardless of their philological evolution, regardless of their past, the dreams we dare to dream die. Robert Frost once said,

"A Poem is Like an Immortal Wound One Never Fully Recovers From."

It might be fair to say this applies really to any narrative written intending to inspire and influence positive change.

Somewhere in the illustrations of these formative years chronicled here that might parallel your own life, for some are dancing in your imagination and burning in your brain this very moment. Your mind's eye, which is also driven by Faith is like a child's and I challenge you before the close of this section to let it explode with unrestrained possibility. What if you could use that very power of inspiration, creation, and connection with everyone you meet? Oh, how you could and would change the world. I may be an artist of written words, to some a charmer with the gift of metaphorical illustrations or a mere creative conjurer of emotion, but the real power is not in the words but from where they are inspired and fashioned. My actions are not what they once were because to utilize the Spirit of Resiliency, I had to change the way I thought. Yes, I said this again because it is the key to true Resiliency.

This seemingly endless canvas that is this very narrative, where the past once visible in black and white; became a place where words live, breathe, evolve and is open to all who will embrace such a truth.

This would refer to believers in Christ, non-believers, artists, inventers, Military Strategists, thinkers, the homeless person on the street corner and any being in this world; hold on longer because you've come this far! You all have value and are worth more than you know! Therefore, regardless of where you are in life or where you have been I will meet you there and even now you are in my prayers, but I am not the only one who will do this and not the important one. So, as I come to the close of this main narrative I have a gift for you, a truth even if you do not believe it. You as well are magical and have the potential to let your light shine before all men. Each person has a gift and you too have the power to create thoughts, feelings, and imagery in people's minds in your own way but first you must change the way you think and see the world. Your actions are the very example of what you believe to be true so guard your mind and your actions will be guarded. Believe in the impossible and the possible will reveal itself. I am not speaking of fantasy or flying horses but of a God who loves you.

I remember listening with a childlike wonder to my former Pastor Rev Hosey on Sunday Morning as the Holy Spirit, The Spirit of Resiliency guided him through powerful thought provoking sermons. A lot of those messages grabbed hold of me with an immense amount of spiritual pressure, and yet, I yearned for the pressure to crush me even harder because in that place of worship God always met and still meets me where I am regardless of where I have been. It is an ongoing relationship that requires on my part a "childlike Faith" that is steadfast and unmovable which believes in miracles and the possibility of the impossible!

Once you dare to believe this like me you will find the waves still rage but you can endure them. Through the belief Jesus Christ died for all men and that His Grace has saved us that sets us free from the past you will find purpose. God helps us discover our passions and unique ways to craft and tell stories that are true. We are human and therefore just ordinary bards of past, present and future dreams.

A story teller of average tales even if it is told only through the actions we reveal. However; if we hope to inspire or be inspired we must believe that Christ takes that ordinary and makes them extraordinary! If you will dare to believe it Jesus Christ will dwell with in you. If you feel the heartstrings of your immortal soul tugging at you right now as my current Pastor, Jade would say, believe in the impossible. Bow your head, descend to your knees. Most likely you are alone right now reading these words and if you are feeling led "Cry out to Jesus" and his "Grace like Rain" will touch you and he will dwell in you. You will feel what I felt many years ago and the very reason I can share this story with you is because somewhere at the intersection where hope and hopelessness met, "*I took the road less traveled by and that made all the difference.*" It was by Faith I stepped up out of the ashes and I know with all my heart anyone reading this can too. It will be hard and not without challenges, but it will change your life! If you are ok with your life, that's wonderful. Yet, if something is missing and you long for the Spirit of Resiliency that saved my life; know you will not face this crusade alone.

My Pastor, when standing before us always emphasizes that though we are ordinary men and women, that Spirit which dwells with in us can do the extraordinary, the unexplainable, the impossible and can move the mountains in any life no matter how big. This story has been about those mountains, the waves upon an unrelenting ocean and yet the Spirit of Resiliency makes those mountains passable and those oceans sailable.

There is one last confession I must make before entering the final section of this book before the inspirational essay's and a few poems to ignite the resilient spirt section. That confession is that just because you Cry out to Jesus in this moment does not mean that the troubles of life magically disappear and should you cry out find a church family or even a prayer warrior to help you grow in the choice and new life you have chosen. There are no strings attached, no buying of forgiveness only faith. Grace, this Author found is receiving something we did not earn or deserve and it was already given for us. Mercy is that which holds back what we do deserve and that too was given when Jesus died on that cross. So, knowing all this even if you choose not to believe such mercy and grace exist, I hope you will continue to the last section.

Food for Thought from the Author

You are almost there and I thank you for those who have come this far with me! This journey, this trek through intersecting lives has taken me almost six years to chronical but what at times feels like a lifetime lived. I hope that the stories of resiliency, the opportunities not taken and the defining moments which have helped me to pen this narrative moved you and tugged at your heart strings regardless of where you are in life or what your values or belief system consists of in this present moment. I have tried to tell not just my story but those of so many in which my life has intertwined and is connected to. They have all good and bad impacted me in an awe-inspiring way. You see I have learned not just from writing this narrative but through many "defining moments" that it is our thoughts which become our obstacles, blocking us, from achieving true happiness and spiritual growth. We become stuck in in the quick sand of saying negative things about ourselves and others causing us to sink deeper into bitterness and brokenness.

Within the corridors of yesterday I have tried to fashion and outline as best I could that while we all have wounds from our past we must not repeatedly ponder about them or linger in those oceans. In doing so we grow weary and by reconnecting ourselves to the pain of yesterday we rob ourselves of the joy that today offers. The truth is as I once discovered by doing this we fashion and place bias and injustice upon ourselves because this action keeps our wounds open and our thoughts focused not on the present.

If you may recall I mentioned earlier that my mother asked me what this narrative was about and I think as I come to the close I know the answer for sure! So, mom if you are reading this here you go. It is all about forgiveness but on many plains across the human landscape! That is how we break every chain. Forgiveness is about the forgiver and by forgiving what has happened you allow the door to open again, cutting the strings that bind you to it and there you move forward. Through the Prophet Isaiah verses 43:25 God reminds us he takes away our transgressions and remembers our sins no more. So why is it, we have such a hard time doing the same? It is simple. We rarely realize until it is too late that the past does not just go away! It must be purified and dealt with effectively. To be free we must deal with our sins, mistakes, pages of history we wish not to read honestly and biblically. I once heard it said,

"*I would rather be an honest mess before God, than a dishonest Saint before men.*" I can tell my readers with certainty, that I my friends am an honest mess.

Finally; I have come to the steadfast understanding I don't care about my imperfections or the world's uncertainty, or the secrets I held onto so long, or anything else that has torn me apart. I don't care about the mistakes I have made, or the words I cannot take back. I do care much about the lessons I have learned; it is all the bad I just don't care about anymore. Do you know why? Because it is all in the past and the past no longer has a hold of me because of what Christ Jesus has reveled in me. I am his no matter what yesterday says and I want you to know today:

Some days are still tough because negative thoughts not forged in truth attempt to bring me back to another time and place. We are all human and it is our very nature to be easily distracted and blown off course. Still each day that the sun rises and my feet, one by one touch the floor, I am reminded through grace and faith that life is a prodigious journey. One which moves towards the destination God has planned for us and if we would dare to believe it we will find within ourselves the same resilient Spirit lives. The Sprit of Resiliency is Christ in us!

If you feel led pray this prayer where you are God will meet you there. If you do not know what you may believe that's ok too because there is no pressure here and no one will know the choice you make except you and God who sees what is unseen and seen. Even in your feelings of unworthiness and brokenness; there is no situation God cannot mend, no life He cannot restore. It does not mean he will fix it like Bob the builder but he we be with you. As sure as the seasons will come and go with each passing year I know this to be true. Living on purpose I have found means taking control of our lives. It means waking up and saying,

"Today, I am going to fight hard to carve out the life I want,"

even when it might be hard to believe or even see. There is no better time than now to draw a line in the sands of the past and move forward right now in in this present moment we know as Today. It truly could be the beginning of the rest of your life. So, if your heart is telling you something is missing I challenge you to step out in faith and sincerely believe this could be "your defining moment" as you pray this prayer or even one of your own.

"Father In heaven, you know my purpose though I may not. You loved me when I did not love myself. You watched and cried with me when I did. Lord, I do not know really the words I am to pray so I simply ask in Jesus Name that you will come into my life and mend my brokenness as only you can. Help me to let go of what I cannot change and give me courage today to feel with in me the Holy Spirit that I may endure, overcome and flow forward like a river. Father I ask in Jesus Name that you would place faithful nonjudgmental Christian friends in front of me to help me grow in the act of faith I have made in this moment. Amen "

I pray that you the reader if it applies realize as I did that our life story is just that, but our autonomy and our futures rests in how we take ownership of it and who we place our faith in. Even if one cannot believe in this present moment, the lessons and stories in the pages before can still be applied to any life regardless of where they are on their journey.

My Serenity Prayer for the Resilient Spirt

God grant me the serenity to accept the people and challenges before me I cannot change, the courage to influence the possibilities of change to those you place in my path, and the wisdom to know that I am the only person I can change for certain.

Lord give me the endurance to soldier through long days and hours whether at work or at school, the fortitude to appear strong even when I am weak and the ability to always love those who may never love me. Father bless the friends I have made and lost through the years, give them fortitude to endure whatever trial they are facing. Bless them and shower them with your "Grace like Rain" when the flames of life burn them where ever they might be. May they always see you through me every day.

To those who have left this world, bless their families and grant them a *"peace which surpasses all understanding."*

Father when I am struggling remind me it is ok to cry and there is no shame in this for even your very son did so on the Cross as he died for me, those I love and those I have yet to meet.
Oh Lord, Father in heaven, Grant me the ability to show my wife through my actions she is the light of my life next to you!
Dear God, I pray you would fill me with your wisdom I might pass it to my sons so I will see them again when my body dies and I walk this earth no more. I lift this to you in Jesus Name.
Father grant me the ability to extend Grace and Mercy no matter who needs it.

Grant me the ability to love others even when they might never love me.
I pray Father you grant me strength when I am weak,
In my victories regardless of how small, Father grant me humility of the heart, that I would never boast.

I will praise you Lord during defeat because I know you will raise me up.
I praise you Father when times are good and harder when it storms! For through my suffering you make me strong and I will praise you for this all my life long.

Lord, I pray you would always guide my feet and keep me from wandering as wandering feet often do,
Please keep on the straight and narrow, because I know *your "eye is always on the sparrow."*

Lord should my wings refuse to soar, give me flight just once more.
May your light dwell in and through me even when days seem dark.

Lord grant me your eyes in Jesus name, so I can see other's the same way as you. In all things big and small, good and bad I praise you and thank you in Jesus Name

-*Amen*

The Walls I Built

I built up walls to guard my heart,
So that no one could destroy me or tear it apart,
Each brick I built from the Fear of Failure and Fears of being left alone,
With the years those walls had grown leaving little room for emotions to roam,

Till one day I looked up to see the walls so high,
That they blotted out the Sun from the sky,
What I was guarding imprisoned me in a self-made tomb of solitude,
I became a walking shell of a person and it appeared there was nothing I could do,

In my weakness I cried out to God from the deepest parts of my soul and being,

"Lord, help me to feel the warmth of your spirit and see the miracle in me you are seeing,
Make me new and unafraid to let those I love and those who love me inside,
Tear these walls down Lord Jesus with your Grace and please let me know it is ok to cry,
Oh Lord Jesus I pray for direction and discernment in line with the Father's Will,
I love you and believe in your healing power still,"

Slowly the walls are falling with each day that is new,
It is still a challenge but God will do what he says he will do,
Jesus said, "And I will do whatever you ask in My name, so that the Father may be glorified in the Son"

Each promise God has made me he has kept each one,

Lord create in me something new,

As only you can do!

All this I pray in Jesus Name,

The same Name that healed the blind and lame

-Amen

Master of Change

"To be a Master of Change one must accept that like their own mortality it is inevitable. Such a Warrior must embrace Change and have the courage to recognize that it is not the enemy but rather an essential alley to the evolution of the human condition as well as the preservation of their immortal soul. "-Clayton Malachi Lynch

We Never See the Storm Coming

We never see the storm coming until we are in its wake,

Battered and beaten it appears this vessel will break,

But I know firsthand that the storms will pass,

They were never meant to last,

And when it feels as though the world makes no sense,

Or like you are being twisted by despair by and aging and rusted wrench,

Soldier onward through those storms for the Son will bring you peace,

For he died for us so sin would now know defeat

Those storms are tests we all must endure,

They are meant for good so we will suffer no more,

Rather they break us down to build us up,

Even when it feels as though we have had enough,

I look back on yesteryear to see days that were filled with grief,

But by God's grace and forgiveness this weary soul found its relief,

So, when the rain pounds away at your aching soul,

Do not let it defeat you or take its toll,

For those who wait and trust in the lord,

Will soar with eagles and be weary no more.

Thoughts of an Overcrowded Mind

As daytime fades with the blinking of an eye,
The moon places himself in the now darkened sky,
As I watch him smiling at the world below,
I wonder does he know something that I do not know?
For my mind is crowded with thoughts of the past,
I look back to see a child made of stain glass.
So easy to break, so easy to forget,
No matter how hard he tried it never seemed his best!
My mind is crammed with thoughts confusing,
Why does the Moon seem to find this amusing?
He did not grow up an outcast child,
Perhaps that is why he can smile?
I see yesteryear as though it were dust,
Still I do not know why it crowds my mind this much!
I see that child breakable as could be,
He was the wax image slash replica of me,
My mind aches as though it has been trampled by a dozen wild stallions
And all around my inner demons are constantly prowling,
I suppose my one hope has been God has promised me,
Everlasting life! He asks only that I believe!
So maybe the Moon smiles because he too knows this truth,
I imagine my real problem is I am so stuck on my youth!
Lord please vanquish this thoughts in an overcrowded mind,
I pray that you would help me to recall a better time.
So now as night fades silently away,
I brace myself with hope of this brand-new day!
For I am confident that the child made of glass,
Is a child I now leave in my past!
For I am living here today and that is where I will dwell,

Instead of circumstances I cannot change I think I have learned this lesson well!

Thank you lord Jesus for living in me and helping me to be all you want me to be,

Thank you for helping me to see I am special and why you died for me.

I am sorry for my selfishness that lingered in my mind,

Over things that happened in another place and time.

I praise you lord from the ends of the earth,

Thank you for helping me to see my worth!

-Amen

A Day through the Eyes of Broken Man

Oh brother, oh sister, you see me standing there,

You are quick to judge me for my uncombed hair,

Oh brother, oh sister, you see me standing there,

You are quick to judge me because of the torn clothing I wear,

On that street corner you are quick to pass me by,

Most days you won't even look me in the eye!

Did you know I was once like you in days when time was young?

Still no one recalls the sacrifice fashioned beneath the scorching sun!

No one remembers that winter when my family thought I had died,

Still you pass me by never looking me in the eye!

I served my country and gave the only thing I could,

On a painted battlefield I once bravely stood,

In my youth I was strong like the old oak tree,

But I have withered and now my countrymen seem to mock me,

Inside it burns; it is a forge of sorrow,

To think that I sacrificed my tomorrow,

So, my country would remain and endure through the storm,

But no one remembers the lives torn,

There quick to attack my PTSD,

But they did not see what I still try not to see!

If you stopped to look in to my eyes,

Perhaps somewhere through those forlorn corridors you would see the man inside,

I was a soldier for my country and my Lord

Though you may not know me I will love both forever more,

Please do not pass me by; please do not judge me,

For though I may seem broken, there is more you see?

I was once young and strong and swift on my feet once before,

I like my brothers marched onward as we stormed those bloody shores,
But how could you understand if you have never seen war
As you sleep peacefully after kissing your children and locking your front door?

Inside my mind the chaos and images are imprisoned in my brain,
Of another place and time which I can no longer name.
As Veterans Day finds its way once more,
Please do not forget what my brothers died for!
They cried on those fields and fell on those shores,
Terrible is the cadence of war!
Oh brother, oh sister, you see me standing there,
Please do not judge me I only ask for your prayers,

A Late-Night Prayer

Dear Father in heaven I am having trouble sleeping,

I do not even know why my heart is aching as it's beating

I know my storms of yesterday are not the storms of today,

The Winds of Life do not blow the same way,

Yesterday the voice of regret whispered in my ears,

The sting of choices made pierced me from other years,

Was not you but the voice of the Evil one

Trying to taunt me with worries of things that will likely never come

Father today I fight to stay above waters that seems to keep rising,

Yet I am stronger than yesterday and this is surprising,

I see in front of me Jesus Christ and am brave until I see the wind so I cry out "help me Lord I am drowning"

Like Peter on that water I find that when the storm is at its worst the problem is in my doubting,

No doubt that Jesus is all He says He is but that He can take me and make me new,

Father I am scarred and torn, worn down and broken, struggling as so many do,

But as the waves and wind thrash and roar, Jesus reaches out his hand and catches me every time when all seems lost,

Time after time your Son picks me up and carries me like that cross,

His burden He willingly carries because of Amazing Grace,

Then in the storms of today I am not a waste of space,

For whatever reason unknown Jesus calms the storms in me,

The ones that tell me,

"you have no purpose, no place in this world, you have no future so run!"

He lifts me up broken and tattered when I feel like I am just done,
I have not lived all that long but Father I think I understand,
That everyone's storms may differ but we can be upheld by the same loving hand,

When the storms of yesterday and those of today drag us into the depths,
We can find comfort in knowing that Jesus Christ will give us rest,
Faith is the connection we can have to the Son and to you oh Father God,

Hope I believe is the light that shines brightest when the storm tries to block it with despairs thick fog,
Yet; the greatest of the three Jesus taught on that cross is unconditional love,

That comes from you oh gracious and merciful Father above,

Father I thank you for watching over me and blessing me when the days have been kind and warm,
I pray your forgiveness in Jesus name for doubting your power to heal and calm this current storm,
I praise you Father for never giving up on me and loving me when I struggle to love my self,
In times of great joy and in times of strife I will turn to you and nothing else,
-Amen

Inner Strength (A Martial Artist's Song)

The road has been difficult, but now your nearly there,
You are more than just a martial artist, musician, or dreamer but also a warrior of prayer,

Black Belts, like baptism are outward symbols of what was already deep inside of you,
Inner strength, endurance courage and the will to push change and become something new,

The hills have been steep, the sweat intense, but the outcome will be worth it you will see,
The journey will continue once you reach the mountain peak, Remain flexible like the bamboo tree,

Learn, and teach, but be willing to inspire through action more than just words,
Inner strength is the ability to do more than just break boards,
It is never giving up on and off the mat,
It is weathering the storms and embracing change regardless of where you are at,

Trust always in God to guide your path as it is so very narrow,
Remember His Eye is always on the Sparrow,
Let faith guide you and wisdom define you,
When it gets difficult and you are growing weary know I am praying that God will pull you through as only he can do.

No Reason Why

I gave my heart, I gave my love, I gave all of me,

Then one day just like that you up and left,

My heart it broke, my love remains, my dreams lost in another time and place,

Looking back asking myself what did I do that created such space,

No real reason, no reason, you said goodbye,

The world spins out of control as a grown man cries,

Then in my brokenness I hear God say,

"Come to me child, come to me and pray,

I might not tell you what you want to hear, I may not fix the circumstance,

Still come my child, because this is the moment that will teach you to dance,

When it rains and when it pours, you will remember what your knees are for,

Give me your heart, give me your love, give me all of you,

I will not leave, I never have, I have been here in the storm,

I am the mender of broken hearts, restorer of dreams, the creator of time and space,

I will tell you where you have fallen short, but I will love you every day,

Come child, pray"

As God's words penetrate the lining of my heart I feel like Im not alone,

No reason, no reason, but even in my sorrow I feel at home,

The world spins out of control but I cannot feel it move,

I Praise God for days he let me spend with you,

Though my heart is shattered like glass,

I am reminded by the hand of God's Grace all the times you made me laugh,

I cannot see tomorrow and I cannot allow myself to drown,
So, when it rains, when it pours, I love you forevermore,
When my heart breaks, when my life shakes, I will remember what my knees are for,

When the Sun Rises in the Eastern Skies, When the Sun Sets and daytime dies,
I will remember what my knees are for as I praise God even if there is no special reason,
Except that He is worthy of such praise and I am not,

When I place my feet on the floor after getting out of bed I will praise him because my heart has not stopped,
No reason, no reason except scars tell stories of Grace and Agape love,

When it rains and when it pours, when the rain becomes a flood,
I will love those who will never love me forever and ever more,
When the sun shines and when it does not, I will remember what my knees are for

In the Eye of The Storm

Yesterday's sky blackened and dark,

It's ocean a shadow because a storm is on the horizon,

The scars of one's youth, a heart torn apart,

As the waves in the distant keep on rising,

The calm seems to come at the center of a storm,

For such times men were born,

To endure through rain, and the darkest of nights,

So, their scars would tell stories of an extraordinary life,

There is no growth without the rain,

There is no healing without the pain,

In the eye of the storm your character is born,

And beyond those clouds there will be a new morn,

When the thunder crashes,

And the vessel thrashes,

Remember your scars tell stories of an extraordinary life,

Stories that to others will become a much-needed light,

So, when the day seems dark and dreary,

There will come a time when you see oh so clearly,

It will be in the eye of the storm,

Where you character and resiliency is born.

I AM

I am a person of hopeful thoughts,

I make the best with all that I've got,

The waves of my soul ripple gently these days,

Even in storms that come my way,

I am a man whose been through many internal wars,

By the Grip of His Grace I am not alone anymore,

I am a person who falls,

As a poet sometimes, I write a bad rhyme,

Still, the scars etched on the canvas of my soul,

Have made me stronger as I grow old,

I try so hard to stay on the straight and narrow,

Because I know "*His Eye Is Always on The Sparrow*,"

I am a person once a prisoner of Time,

Through grace I am no longer a detainee of my own mind,

I find joy in living and thank God for each sunrise,

At night before going to sleep I talk to him as I close my eyes,

Then as the heavier lights of the outside world dim,

In my dreams as I sleep I see myself on the back of the wind,

Carrying me to places I never thought I could go,

Like I river moving forward I see my self-flow,

No longer standing still or going back

I am a person now above that,

I am a person of hopeful thoughts,

Thankful to God for the battles once fought,

So, if you are in the storm so to speak,

Take heart and throw yourself at Jesus's feet.

I Will Be a River

Finally, I understand there are three main days in our lives,

Yesterday, today and tomorrow, thanks to the newfound strength I have inside,

Of those three days only one really matters to me,

Yesterday I left in the storms of a troubled sea,

Tomorrow is always one step ahead of me,

Therefore, it is Today that truly sets me free,

The Spirit of God is as a river flowing through me,

Even in darkness I am reminded that He guides my destiny,

He is always moving forward, never going back and never stands still,

My past no longer defines me even if it did help to shape me,

I have learned to dance in the hallways of life when God closes doors,

Because the plans He has for me will open others to something more,

Today I will be a river never going back, never standing still, but always moving forward,

In every life there are moments of doubt, fear, and uncertainty,

It is human nature and easy to drown and become lost at sea,

Lord knows I have been through Fire and Rain,

It is because of those moments I am no longer the same,

Once stuck, trapped by memories of another time,

It took Resiliency, a Spirit With in and compass guiding my soul and my mind,

I will be a river always moving forward, never again will I go back or stand still,

Every morning I place my feet on the floor,

I will thank God for opening Today's door,

And should the sunset upon my life,

I pray those who remember and loved me will share that light,

To you my readers be like a river, do not go back, do not stand still, move forward,

Longfellow and I

Longfellow once penned such beautiful lines, that pierced souls and penetrated so many minds,

Longfellow and I would be such great friends,

Because both of us long for "Peace on earth and Good Will to Men"

"O souls amid earth's busy strife, The Word of God is light and life;

Oh, hear His voice, make Him your choice, Hail peace on earth, good will to men."

I pray this Christmas season, that we all remember that God's son is the reason,

When we stand beneath newly fallen snow,

May the world see through us Christ's loving glow,

Oh When we "bow our heads in despair" let us remember that God hears our prayers,

As Christmas Day makes its round in the year 2019 AD,

Let us look back on the year with praise thanking God for bringing us to this point unscathed,

Let us thank Him for the trials that made us stronger

For the Faith that pushed us a little bit longer,

My prayer for the world is just as Longfellow penned,

That the true meaning of Christmas will help broken hearts to mend,

Our hearts will melt and lives will change,

"Then happy, singing on your way,

Your world will change from night to day;

Your heart will feel the message real,

Of peace on earth, good will to men."

Breath of Inspiration

Where does creativity find its beginning when all you have is a dream?
What is the special element that turns mere words into people, places
and things?
As a poet and dreamer, I've been asked this many times,
See, people don't understand how I can fashion such emotion in written
lines,
When I close my eyes and say my prayers,
My inspiration seems to come from there!
The life thus far that I have called my own helps to pave my way,
The past has become a tool to help me say what I want to say,
There is inspiration inside of every human heart,
Many of them just know not where to start,
Some don't care because they live for them self,
So, their mind-set is simply "why care about anyone else?"
The breath of inspiration whether a poet, artist, or simply musician,
Is breathed from the mind's eye and placed into its designated position
Whether it be metaphors created for a specific reason,
Or a certain color to surface a certain season,
All is created with gifts God has given,
I give credit to him for every word I've ever written,
So, who am I who can fashion such emotion?
Who am I who puts poetry into motion?
I am only a humble writer, who dreams of inspiration,
I am only a weaver of feelings and written formation,
I remember being five and hating the world around me,
My dream was to morph into an eagle so I could fly free,
The use of child-hood abuse was my safety net and crutch,
Yet as I got older and wiser I couldn't rely on it much,
See, God had a plan I just had to let go of it all,
Be willing to let him pick me up each time I would fall,

So, it was that my thoughts became words and words published print,

It was testimony to others as well as spiritual hints,

The breath of inspiration begins with the individual himself,

After he finds his place, he can inspire everyone else!

An Author's Prayer

I am blessed to be alive and share these thoughts with you,

As thanksgiving approaches I brace myself because another year is upon me too,

There is so much to be thankful for,

I have said this so often but I must say it once more,

If we wake to the rising of another sun and the day has found us with care,

Then truly we are blessed should we make it there,

For tomorrow is a dream that never really comes true,

It does not exist and so today is what starts us anew,

I am thankful for each of my days though I know I am not worthy of them,

I am thankful for all of you my family and many friends,

My prayer is that people will understand how fragile this life can be,

If they do not believe this than look at me,

I have stared at death as he has called out my name,

Though I did not fear him I heard him all the same,

In a wink a blink a glance of a brief glimpse all might fade away,

At any time, we might be called for here on earth we were not meant to stay,

My prayer is that we all might be thankful for what lies before us,

And except that what God has given is more than enough,

I pray with all the prayer that I have,

That in this short life we might all find reason to be glad,

I pray that we might leave the past where it lay,

And in doing so thank God that we woke up today,

I felt the need to speak through this rhyme,

Because too often we do not see the blessings we chose to leave behind,

Be ever so thankful for all that you are given,

Take joy in the gift of praise and worshiping God for therefore we are living,

I did not always believe as I do,

But like the four seasons souls can change too,

I am thankful for a God who will take me as I am,

Just one who loves him and all of you simply an ordinary man

My Mother's Choice

The days have swiftly morphed into fading years,

And now the third decade of my life draws ever so near,

As I glance back through those corridors of my life,

I see with aging wisdom many left turns that should have veered right,

Yet, I am blessed because you often held my hand,

When I stumbled which was often you helped me to stand,

As the mountains so frequently pierced the clouds of an uncertain life,

You told me to trust in the Lord Jesus Christ,

When I could not hold back tears forming in my crestfallen eyes,

You reminded and assured me that men could cry,

Did not Jesus cry on that rugged cross,

As he loved and prayed for the broken and lost?

You taught me that he was more than a man, but God's beloved son,

As I am yours until the final cadence of life's pounding drum,

So often I thank God that you never gave in,

I know I pushed you to the brink to the brim,

But you showed me that love is something one does,

It is not just an action but a choice to love,

Love is unconditional it does not fail,

Even through the storms and hail,

It never boasts or brags about what it has done,

You loved me and hugged me and called me your son,

You held me accountable for my choices made,

But you always said I love you before the end of each day

I am honored to tell folks you are my mother,

I pray for you always thanking God that for this moment how ever so brief we have each other.

Blood Shed Tears

(For all those who sacrificed their tomorrows, so that others might live
to see theirs)

I stand on a field all drenched in red,

Many have fallen and my best friend is dead!

As lightning races through the night sky,

I cry out to God, because this soldier isn't ready to die.

All I can see is a sky highlighted with black smoke,

I only pray that Lisa Marie got that last letter I wrote.

For if God's plan is that I am to die,

Then I will not question him, I just don't want Lisa to cry.

So, I told her "Baby I'm doing just fine."

It's a good thing that she doesn't know I'm far behind enemy lines.

Tracers and missiles go streaming past my head and a stray bullet
kisses my side,

Oh, merciful Lord please let this soldier stay alive.

Cannons are roaring and death seems to be calling,

One by one brave men and my nation are still falling.

Another bullet tears deep into my skin,

I can't bare it and so I fall to the earth calling out to "Him."

Dear father in heaven please help me because your soldier is fading fast!

This next breath might be his last.

All I can see is the blood, tears and pain,

You know all Lord; so, I reckon you are aware that I feel the same!

I'm trying my best lord to stop all my crying,

Still I know that the hour is upon me and I am dying.

Please tell my family I love them all.

Please dear God tell them why I took this fall.

Tell America why we all died.

Please dear God don't forget all the tears we cried.

Please dear Lord, keep this country of mine free.

If not for them, please do it for me.

I've done your will in all my days,

In this final hour father, I tried my hardest to be brave!

Many more will fall I'm sure.

Please tell them we're sick of the hatred and we don't want to fight anymore.

God please dry these blood shed tears,

I know my prayers have kissed your ears.

Forgive me oh father of my many sins,

I'll know in a few seconds if you're going to let me in.

Love me dear father as I now rest my eyes,

Love always your soldier Captain Malachi McBride.

It's December

It's December and the days are growing much colder,

Time doesn't care about me because I'm still growing older.

I used to think that time was on my side,

Yet in a single wink it only faded further from my eye.

It's December and another year is almost through,

It's eccentric how things tend to alter from what we once knew.

I can recall playing in the high school Jazz Band,

Now I am no longer the one they once called the Trumpeter Blues Man.

It's December, Father Winter is back once more,

Soon we will decorate and hang wreathes upon our front door.

I finally understand that we fade away with each New Year,

I can still see high school graduation and the fear of not knowing my set career.

It's December and people I knew are still changing,

Just Like me and all those things I've been naming.

I can feel life rushing swiftly by,

Like a rollercoaster all one can do is hold on for the ride.

The stars didn't shine when I was nine and ten,

The reason I reckon, is that I never took the time to notice them.

I let so many opportunities run away from my life,

Somewhere along the way I just lost sight.

It's December and I've come to understand,

That life is what we make it and the choices we make lie in the palm of our hand.

I have learned that Time is no one's ally or lost friend,

Time only mocks us when we are at the weaker end.

So live life to the fullest one day at a time,

Most importantly bare this lesson in your mind.

It's December and the days are growing much colder,

Time doesn't care because I'm still growing older

Let Me Be a Lighthouse

I want to stand on the tallest cliff so that my light may shine brighter than bright.
It is my sincere aspiration and ambition that others might know Jesus Christ.
I want to share all that I have in the hope others might do the same.
It is my greatest wish that people will commit all they do in Jesus' holy name.
I see so many souls lost in the oceans of transgression and confusion.
It is my most genuine prayer that I can win them away from Satan's many illusions.
I want to be a lighthouse whose faith can guide lost ships home.
It is with an undeniable yearning I hope to convince them that they are never alone.
Let me be a lighthouse oh Lord whose love might guide them to you.
Give me the courage to see into people's hearts so that I will know what to do.
Let me be strong when the oceans become fierce and storm clouds invade my life.
Give me that fortitude dear God to live by example and role model by following the teachings of Christ.
Let all that I am Lord be a delight in your eyes and please guide me every day.
Give me that endurance father to teach non- believers how to pray.
Let my life be a testimony so that others might learn of the legitimacy you speak.
Give me patience father when I begin to grow weak.
I know sometimes folks are led astray by scientific results.
In some circumstances they have learned to view all religions as cults.
I know that some people feel as though God could never ever love them.
In many lives they're too afraid to call out to him.

I want to prove to them all, that faith is powerful and can change a person's heart.

In the good book, faith is how a lot of the scriptures start.

I long to share with them why Jesus' hung on that cross and died.

In all essence I want to be a lighthouse that guides them to everlasting life.

Let me be a lighthouse whose light shines with the light of the Holy Ghost.

Give me the words dear father when I need them most.

Let me rest peacefully Lord for tomorrow will be another long day.

Give me the correct answers oh God when a seeker asks, "how should I pray?"

Let me be your lighthouse guiding those lost ships away from the rocks.

Give me serenity when all the doors have been met with locks.

Let me be all that you want me to be and all while doing what's right.

Give me mercy and grace as I continue to live a Christian life.

I want to stand on the tallest cliff so that my light may shine brighter than bright.

It is my deepest aspiration and ambition that others might know Jesus Christ.